## "Don't turn on the light."

Remi was standing in the doorway to the living room, the faint glow from the streetlights outside outlining her body. The skirt and blouse she had been wearing had been exchanged for a robe that barely covered her thighs and clung to her body the way Dominic longed to do.

"I...I didn't thank you for rescuing me," she said. "You saved my life."

"Your gratitude is not necessary." God's teeth, *how he wanted her!*

She came toward him, stopping beside his bed. "Yes, it is necessary," she insisted. "I can only imagine what might have happened if you hadn't been there."

"I only regret that I did not arrive sooner. If I hadn't been so stubborn...." Then he made the fatal mistake of touching his finger to her mouth. And the truth poured out of him with a stream of emotion that threatened to become a riptide.

"I was jealous." His fingertip skimmed across her bottom lip. "The thought of another man touching you sent me into a rage. I had no right to think of you as mine, but I did. God help me, I still do."

Dear Reader,

Knights in shining armor, damsels in distress, magic spells and chants—the stuff of every little girl's dreams, right? Right. And some big girls', too. I'm not too proud to admit that I've always harbored a secret desire to live in Camelot. Who hasn't?

Naturally, when the editors at Temptation gave me the opportunity to contribute to the ROGUES miniseries, it was simply too good to pass up. So I charged my crystal ball, put fresh batteries in my magic wand and off I went. Over the rainbow and smack-dab into some of the best fun I've had in…well, I can't remember when.

I hope you'll enjoy meeting *The Knight* as much as I did. He's tall, dark and handsome and has a Lancelot complex that won't quit. What more could any damsel ask?

Happy Reading,

Sandy Steen

# THE KNIGHT
## Sandy Steen

*Harlequin Books*

TORONTO • NEW YORK • LONDON
AMSTERDAM • PARIS • SYDNEY • HAMBURG
STOCKHOLM • ATHENS • TOKYO • MILAN
MADRID • WARSAW • BUDAPEST • AUCKLAND

For all the damsels who have a "knight in shining armor"
in their own living room
and just don't recognize him

ISBN 0-373-25693-0

THE KNIGHT

# ROGUES

# ROGUES ACROSS TIME

---

## THE KNIGHT

The knights of old were men of honor and chivalry. Their deeds were legendary, their bravery inspiring. These men were fiercely loyal to king and country and upheld a unique and stringent code of honor unlike any the world had known before, or since. They represent a time in history that has come to symbolize the kind of nobility men still seek, but seldom find.

Sir Dominic Longmont was a knight of the realm and vassal to the Duke of Kerwick. As a warrior of uncommon bravery during the last battles of the Wars of the Roses in 1485, he supported Henry Tudor's claim to the throne of England. Longmont was the leader of a valiant, but ill-fated force separated from the main battle at Bosworth Field. He survived and was later instrumental in saving the life of Henry the Seventh.

# 1

*The Past*
*England, August 22, 1485*

AMID THE FADING SOUNDS of clanking swords and the muted cries of dying men, Dominic William Longmont ripped his helmet from his sweat-drenched head and closed his eyes, gratefully lifting his face heavenward to savor the first drops of a welcome rain and a momentary lull in the fighting. Completely at odds with the heat and hostility of battle, the rain was lavishly cool on his skin. For a moment, he could almost imagine he was somewhere else. But only for a moment.

Dominic opened his eyes and the illusion of serenity vanished. The dead knight at his feet, whose tunic was emblazoned with the white rose of the House of York, and stained bright red with fresh blood, wasn't imagination. Or the others like him, their bodies like broken chess pieces, littering the field just outside the familiar walls of Kerwick Castle. Nor were the faint but still-audible sounds of his men driving back a determined contingent of Richard the Third's forces imaginary. They were all too real.

"Is it ended, my lord?"

Dominic turned to find his squire, Erik, only a few feet away. The lad was new to battle, and though stouthearted and loyal, he was clearly terrified.

"Nay," Dominic answered, wishing he could say otherwise. He looked back at the woods into which Richard's men had disappeared only moments ago. If he looked hard enough, he could catch glimpses of the banners of England and St. George through the trees. "They will redeploy their forces and send forth another wave of bowmen and billmen."

*More killing. For England. For honor.*

"Soon, my lord?"

Standing there in the rain, the squire looked so young, much more so than his fifteen years, and he was so obviously struggling to be brave that Dominic was tempted to lie, if only to give the boy a brief respite from fear. But what good were lies? Dominic knew not how the larger group of men fared against King Richard's forces at Bosworth Field or Redmore Plain, but here, in this small pocket of resistance, the tide of battle had turned against the supporters of the contender, Henry Tudor.

"Aye," Dominic told the steadfast Erik. "Soon."

The squire pulled his rain-soaked cloak tighter around his shoulders. "I fear the weather has turned against us, as well, my lord."

Dominic only nodded. As abruptly as it had come, the summer shower had changed, transforming into a vicious thunderstorm, clouds roiling, swirling black, green and gray into an angry mass of darkness. The rain went from soft to savage, stinging his skin, pelting his armor.

The young aide surveyed the heavens. "Black as a witch's heart, sire."

Dominic glanced heavenward. *A witch's heart indeed.* The sky was now tinged in a strange, ghastly shade of green with only flashes of jagged white lightning to rip and challenge the darkness. The night had been a boon to his small force so familiar with the area, but not enough of a boon, he feared. His losses were heavy, his men discouraged.

Sounds of renewed battle warred with the rising volume of the storm, and emerged victorious. The lull was over.

"Bring Navarr to me," Dominic ordered, and the squire hurried to obey. He glanced toward the sky. This night was meant for death and dying.

"A night conjured straight from the depths of hell," he whispered.

*The Present*
*Dallas, Texas, August 22, 1996*

"ONE HELL OF A NIGHT," Maria Remington Balfour whispered, gazing out the office window of Clint Hogan, Swords and Shields' head knight and trainer. A wicked-looking streak of lightning flashed across the heavens, accompanied by a booming blast of thunder. Remi, as everyone but her parents called her, drew back, then twisted the wand to close the mini-blinds covering the window. She shivered.

What had been a gentle summer shower only moments earlier had suddenly turned into a savage thunderstorm. The sky was an ugly black and green color, the darkness lanced by sharp cracks of thunder and vicious gashes of lightning. And some of those gashes seemed to be perilously close to the Swords and Shields parking lot. The weather had already prevented two employees from showing up at the medieval-style dinner theater, and it would definitely cut into the attendance numbers for tonight's performance. As assistant general manager standing in for the general manager on vacation, it was Remi's job to worry about those numbers.

Clint had sent word that he needed to speak to her before the performance, but as yet, he hadn't shown up. Absently, she pleated the hem of the hip-length silk veil attached to her headpiece. "Oh, stop it," she muttered to herself, irritated that she had never been able to master the nervous habit that had persisted from childhood. Stepping away from the window, she smoothed the folds of her elaborate sorceress's costume and checked her watch. "Way to go. You were about to portray a fifteenth-century sorceress wearing a watch. Not cool."

As she unfastened the slim gold band and slipped it into the voluminous right pocket of her skirt, young Andy Collins, the part-time mail boy, poked his head through the partially open office door.

"Oh, hi. Sorry. I was looking for Clint." His head disappeared, then reappeared so fast it was a blur. "Oh, yeah, since you're here," he said, easing the rest of his lanky frame through the door. "This came for you." His long legs took him across the floor in two strides, and he plopped a shoe-box-size package down on Clint's desk. "That's the second package for you in two days." He grinned, rocking back and forth on his feet as if he had just discovered a secret. "Must be your birthday or something, huh?"

"Or something." She smiled, leaning forward in order to read the return address on the package.

Although Tina, the actress she was replacing tonight, wasn't exactly flat-chested, the bodice of the costume hadn't been cut with Remi's voluptuous figure in mind. She straightened her shoulders, unconsciously causing the fabric of the already snug bodice to stretch even tighter across her breasts.

"Uh...uh, that costume sure looks better on you than it does on Tina."

"Thanks." Remi glanced up in time to see Andy swallow hard, his gaze fixed on her chest.

"Will you find Clint and tell him I'll meet him at the entrance to the arena?"

"Huh?" Andy jerked his gaze up to meet hers.

"Tell Clint I'll—"

"Oh, yeah. Sure. I'll tell him," the red-faced teenager stammered, moving backward toward the door. "Thanks, I mean, excuse me, I mean, see ya later, Miz Balfour." He quickly closed the door behind him.

Remi sighed and shook her head. When it came to a choice between boobs and brains, men were as predictable as the sunrise. Not that she had a vast amount of experience with men. None, in fact, unless she counted the Egyptology student of her father's who had reluctantly volunteered to take her to her prom. What a disaster that had been. Afterward, she hadn't given much serious consideration to men until she was out of college and on her own. But then, most of the men she found truly interesting were either already married or too old to be contenders. She kept her dates friendly, usually ending up with more of a platonic rather than a romantic relationship. Remi knew it was an old-fashioned concept, strictly out-of-date, but she had decided to keep her heart and her body as a gift for the man she would fall in love with.

Hopefully, that day would arrive before she was too old to appreciate it.

She glanced again at the package, an obvious reminder that another year had gone by with her still holding on to her "gift."

*Oh, well* . . . Her fingers automatically traced the thin cotton cord that bound the kraft paper covering the box. The barely legible scrawl and return address assured her the package was from her brother, Mark, currently living in England doing research for his next archaeological dig.

Show time was only minutes away. "I don't really have time to open this." Her fingers lightly drummed the top of the package. "Oh, what the hell," she muttered, ripping at the paper until the box was opened to reveal two books, both about the size of a paperback novel, one thinner than the other.

Although they were undoubtedly antique volumes, she had to smile at the very modern yellow Post-it notes stuck to the front of each book. The first one was entitled *Rogues Across Time*, and the square yellow note read:

Knew you had to have this. You always did have a thing for rogues. Check out the medieval section.

Unable to resist a hurried glance, Remi picked up the book. Strange, she thought, fanning through the whisper-thin pages, the book felt warm to the touch. She continued glancing through it until an illustration of a knight in full armor caught her eye. "Whoa," she whispered.

The man in the black-and-white sketch was tall, broad-shouldered and strikingly handsome. A thick mane of hair fell almost to his shoulders, swept back from his face on one side as though the knight stood against a stout wind. The look in the man's eyes—unreasonably she decided they were a startlingly clear blue—was as hard as the line of his jaw. If the artist had intended to convey the image of a man of strength and power, he had succeeded.

Remi stared at the drawing, mesmerized by the figure of the dashing knight. He looked powerful, even dangerous. Too dangerous, maybe. To dragons and damsels alike. A woman could get lost in those eyes and learn to depend on those strong arms. He certainly looked as if he could fill the bill for a knight in shining armor. Certainly Remi's requirements. The kind of man every girl dreams about. The kind Remi had dreamed about on more than one occasion.

Absently, almost like a caress, she ran her fingertips over the drawing and unexpectedly experienced a strange vibration. Must be the knights on horseback, she thought, coming through the tunnel on their way to the arena. Their hooves on the concrete ramp not far from Clint's office often reverberated through the stone walls. She traced her finger over the knight's face and got a little shock, like static electricity.

"Oh-h-h." She jerked her hand back. "Serves you right for daydreaming." She slapped the book shut. Hadn't she done enough of that as a kid?

As an offspring of eccentric parents who lived a gypsy life-style and dabbled in everything from archaeology to zoo keeping, Remi knew all about daydreams and fantasies. Her childhood had been a series of adventures in one exotic location after another, dealing with one set of out-of-the-ordinary circumstances after another. The other children she encountered thought her life glamorous and enticing, while Remi thought it transient and fragile. Now, all that remained of that vagabond existence were memories, some sweet, some not so sweet. And daydreams, always daydreams—a legacy from her parents' fertile imaginations and their insatiable quest to see what lay just over the next mountain, across the next river. But she was no longer a child, and an unbalanced, unpredictable life was the last thing she wanted now. And that went double for daydreams.

She picked up the second book, stacking it on top of the book of rogues. The leather-bound cover, worn smooth with age, felt almost like satin beneath her fingertips. The yellow note stuck to the cover read:

Found this in a little cubbyhole of a bookstore that I would have had to drag you out of. Some sort of Druid/Celtic weird stuff that you can sort of read but all sounds like Greek to me. How about conjuring me up a truckload of grant money for my next project?

Remi opened the book. As a student of history, particularly medieval, she recognized what were indeed Druid writings. Chants of some kind.

Another double whammy of lightning and thunder pounded the night and Remi glanced at the clock. She didn't have enough time to take the books back to her own office before show time. Oh, well, she'd just have to take them with her until after the performance.

As she proceeded to tuck the volumes into a pocket within the folds of her flowing skirt, she glanced down at the book of chants on top and an intriguing idea popped into her head.

"If I have to play a sorceress, why not make it sound authentic." Satisfied with her stroke of brilliance, she crossed to the door and switched off the light, plunging the room into darkness. Outside, the night sky was black as the devil's soul one second, then seared with a heavenly white as lightning streaked the darkness the next.

*The Past*

THE SKY WAS ALIVE with lightning. Long fingers of white heat raked the night like demons clawing to be free from hell. And hell was exactly where Dominic intended to send the enemies of the soon-to-be Tudor king. Enemies who even now made their way through the woods surrounding Kerwick Castle, drawing ever closer, coming to meet their fate.

The squire returned, a cloak draped over his arm and leading his lord's great war-horse, Navarr. Black as a moonless night, the powerful stallion was more than a magnificently trained animal; he was as much a warrior as Dominic in his own right. They were, in a way, kindred spirits. A gift from the Duke of Kerwick, Navarr was worth a king's ransom. But the duke had always been generous with his money, even with his time. Generous with everything except the one thing that mattered most to Dominic. Now, as he faced what might be his last hour, it was the one thing Dominic knew he would never have.

The Duke of Kerwick's name.

Navarr snorted, tossing his head, almost as if he could sense his master's tension and the anticipation of death. Dominic took the cape from his squire, flung it in a wide swirl around his shoulders, then fastened it with the huge falcon's-head pin the boy handed him. The silver ring he wore on the little finger of his right hand was a miniature of the expertly crafted falcon's head. The carving was the emblem of the Kerwick name and even though it was not his to claim by birth, he had claimed it by honor.

Considered an outlaw knight by some, he, more than most perhaps, knew the value of honor. Because he had made a place for himself among honorable men where there had been none. Since the day his mother had given him the ring upon their arrival at Kerwick Castle from France, he had fought to make her and his father, albeit unrecognized, proud. His entire life was founded on honor. Without it, life was pointless.

He wore no man's colors save his own, though privately he had sworn loyalty to Kerwick. Black chain mail over black leather. The only thing of significance on his teardrop shield was the bar sinister that stated his position to the world. He had been born a bastard, and it appeared he would die a bastard.

"A moment, sire." Erik scooped up the previously discarded helmet and handed it to his knight.

Helmet in hand, Dominic mounted Navarr, wheeling the massive animal to face their adversaries. Then, whether in prayer or frustration, he drew his sword and raised it to the heavens.

*Present*

IN THE DARKENED ARENA the third part of the program, a mock battle loosely imitating the Wars of the Roses, was ready to begin. Music filled the darkness, then crescendoed to a breath-catching pause. There was a blare of trumpets, then suddenly a single spotlight illuminated a golden ring at one end of the arena. Remi stood alone in the ring, smoke clinging to the hem of her costume, now topped with a stunningly beautiful cape studded with faux diamonds, emeralds, rubies and sapphires that glittered and danced in the light.

A murmured *oooh* swept through the crowd. Arms outstretched, Remi turned full circle, her magnificent cape swirling around her, causing tentacles of smoke to coil in the air like thin white serpents. More *ooohs* from the audience. She folded her arms across her chest, tucking her hands inside her voluminous sleeves. The music swelled again. Trumpets blared. Cymbals crashed. In one spectacular gesture, Remi lifted her hands in the air, producing a glistening crystal ball, glowing from within, in one hand, a lighted wand in the other and, as if by magic, she rose several feet from the arena floor.

The crowd cheered and whistled their enjoyment.

With a wave of Remi's wand, spotlights fell on four mounted knights positioned several yards behind her. The knights were in full battle dress bearing the emblem of a white rose signifying the House of York and Richard the Third's forces. Remi then pointed to the other end of the arena, and the spotlight followed, illuminating four more mounted knights in full battle dress but bearing the emblem of Henry Tudor and the House of Lancaster, a red rose.

With the audience's attention focused elsewhere, Remi switched off the battery-powered wand and tucked it back into its hiding place within her sleeve. Then she reached into her pocket for the book of chants, prepared to add the authentic words to her scripted performance. Since she couldn't tell which book was which by their size, she pulled out both. Then finding the book of chants, she placed it on top of the other and opened it. As she did, Remi felt a strange sensation. The books seemed to tingle beneath her fingers. Must be vibrations from the platform, she decided and focused on her performance.

As she floated on her invisible platform over to one side of the arena, the knights began to move.

"War—" her voice resonated from well-placed high-tech sound equipment as she swept the air with the hand holding the crystal ball "—covers the land like a blight, as foretold by the ancient ones. Now brave knights battle to the death. A kingdom is the prize."

With hooves thundering, the mighty war-horses carried forth the two sets of knights, then were reined in, poised and waiting for the mock battle to begin.

"I must have a great and valiant knight to champion the cause," Remi told her audience. "One courageous knight must come forth. A bold hero. Oh, ancient ones, send him to me."

Remi lifted the glowing crystal ball above her head, special-effects lightning dancing around her like fairies in a ring. "Come forth, Gallant One. Come. Come..."

*The Past*

HIS SWORD POISED for battle, Dominic had just urged Navarr forward, when he heard the woman's voice. It seemed to come from far away. The words were distant, soft as wind through the trees, yet he could hear them as clearly as if she stood next to him.

*...a knight to champion the cause.*

Dominic yanked Navarr to a halt. The war-horse half reared, his powerful forelegs thrashing, hooves slicing through the air. The helmet fell from Dominic's grasp, hit the ground and rolled into the darkness. He glanced around. "Who speaks?"

*A bold hero... Send him to me.*

Had some maid wandered onto the battlefield unaware? "Identify yourself, mistress," Dominic demanded. And though he saw no woman, the voice grew stronger, not in volume, but in power. Even the crack of thunder couldn't obliterate the compelling words that were becoming clearer and clearer...

*My lord of honor. Brave and fearless knight, come to me. Come to me. Hear me, valiant knight as I speak the ancient words. I call to you.*

Then abruptly the words changed, became unrecognizable. The strange-sounding language was melodic, with an alluring rhythm, an irresistible cadence. The words vibrated in his soul like a newly struck tuning fork. With each second, the mysterious voice called more strongly to him, swirling around him, enfolding him.

A fleeting thought crossed his mind that he had somehow fallen under a spell. Was he bewitched? If he was, so be it. He could not deny the siren's command any more than he could deny the beating of his heart. He *must* go to her, *must* ride forth into battle. With a mighty war cry, Dominic again raised his sword and spurred his steed.

Suddenly, an eerie blaze of blue-white lightning ripped the night sky, its veiny fingers reaching down for his sword. The bolt struck the metal in a shower of sparks, sending the charge whipping through his body; sending him whirling, spinning, spinning toward the ever-insistent voice...

*Present*

AS REMI SPOKE the last words of the ancient chant, lightning slashed across the arena, and mini-explosions of pyrotechnic colors lit up the ceiling. Bursts of brilliant red and dazzling white sparkled for seconds, then disappeared in puffs of smoke. Starlights of twinkling silver and blue hung suspended for a heartbeat, then cascaded to earth like tiny falling stars.

With another sweeping gesture, Remi turned and pointed. Instantly, the spotlight left her, skimming over the knights, now fully launched in mock combat, to focus on a thick cloud of smoke that appeared to rise mysteriously from the floor of the arena.

Then, an eerie—and unprogrammed—blaze of blue-white lightning ripped through the air, striking the ground and charging the smoke with electricity. The air fairly crackled with it.

Unexpectedly, Remi's entire body began to tingle as if the vibrations from the lightning were zinging through her blood.

The audience held its collective breath.

Remi, too, waited, watching the special-effects smoke screen, expecting the emergence of the star of the show, Paul Tinsdale, the Black Knight.

# 2

CLOAK STREAMING behind him, his weapon at the ready, Dominic bolted through the cloud of smoke like an avenging angel. His head still ringing with the woman's voice, the din of sword against sword, knight against knight, surrounded him. Instinctively moving into the heart of the fight, he swung hard. The shield covering his left forearm struck another knight in the chest. With a surprised grunt of pain, the knight flew off his horse and landed in the dirt.

From out of nowhere a boisterous cheer rang in Dominic's ears. Startled, he reined in Navarr, and glanced around. His eyes widened in shock.

He was no longer outside the castle walls, he was . . . in the courtyard? He looked up. There was no sky. Only a ceiling with some manner of strange rafters. And no rain. There were lights. Everywhere. And . . . people! Hundreds of them!

Where were the castle walls, which only moments ago had been close enough for him to touch? Where were his men? His enemies? Was this a dream? Everything seemed so . . . unnatural. And if he wasn't dreaming, where was this place? And how did he—

Before he could complete the thought, a knight, brandishing a sword and carrying a shield emblazoned with a white rose, thundered toward him on his mount. In a heartbeat, Dominic forgot the mysterious crowd of people and the lights. His fears and questions vanished, and his warrior's instinct took over. He braced himself for a fight to the death.

The knight bore down, wildly swinging his sword. So wildly, in fact, that for a fleeting second Dominic wondered if the man was demented. As his enemy drew even on his right side, Dominic raised his sword, slashed and missed. The Yorkist knight wheeled his horse around as if to make another pass. Then a knight wearing a red rose badge signifying the contender's forces appeared on Dominic's left. A comrade in arms! he thought, but the fellow knight rode directly toward the Yorkist, and engaged in battle, completely ignoring Dominic.

But honor would not be denied. Encircled by battling knights, but without an opponent of his own, Dominic spurred Navarr forward into the fray. He approached one of Richard's men on horseback and a comrade knight on the ground, intending to aid the unhorsed fighter, but before he could wield his sword, a second enemy knight rode up behind him. Dominic turned to face the new threat, and found himself caught between the two. With a mighty war cry, he lunged for the newcomer.

The Yorkist knight jerked hard on the reins in an effort to get out of the way, just as Dominic's sword clanged against his shield. "Hey, man!" the knight called out. "Take it easy!"

"Coward!" Dominic shouted, turning, recklessly plunging forward for a renewed attack.

"What the hell do you think—" The Yorkist knight stopped in midsentence as he looked over Dominic's right shoulder. "Hey! Look out!"

From out of nowhere, another knight galloped into the fray, and before any of the three could prevent it, riders and horses collided. One of the horses screamed, and reared, its powerful hooves pawing the air. Dominic pulled hard on Navarr's reins. Nostrils flared, sides heaving with the effort, the big stallion tried to work free, but couldn't. In the middle of the entanglement, the other horse reared again, thrashing its hooves.

One moment Dominic thought he was free of the melee, the next minute a blinding pain exploded in his head. Then nothing. Blackness.

"YOU'RE GOING to be fine."

That voice! The same one he'd heard before the lightning struck. Now it called to him from a tiny speck of white light in an ocean of blackness. Dominic struggled to reach the light, but it was so far away, and his body felt so heavy. Yet, he knew he *must* keep trying, or the cloying darkness would smother him.

Something cool touched his forehead.

Determined, he fought for consciousness, propelling himself up, and into the light. And like a man finally breaking the surface after being trapped underwater, he filled his lungs with sweet, life-affirming breath, and opened his eyes.

A woman was leaning over him. Smiling, she removed a damp cloth from his forehead. "Welcome back."

Even though the woman was unfamiliar, his surroundings at least were not. Dominic realized he was lying on a narrow cot in one of the castle's anterooms. Or was he? There was something strange about the room. The stone walls were the same, yet he could never remember them appearing so clean. And there were no rushes on the floor; instead, the area was covered in some manner of smooth, flat stone he had never seen before. The wall opposite the end of the bed held one long, wide shelf, and above it were cupboards holding bottles and jars. And the candles in the wall sconces burned, but the flames did not flicker. It was all real, yet unreal. Was he dreaming?

He touched his chest, and discovered that his armor and chain mail had been removed, leaving him only in his leathers. And his sword was gone.

In an attempt to rise, he shifted on the cot, and was rewarded with a throbbing pain on the side of his head. *God's teeth!* He touched the spot then looked at his hand. There were no bandages. No blood. Obviously he had been hit in the head and knocked out; thankfully, his injury must not be severe. A blessing, considering he was uncertain where he was or exactly what had happened. Or the identity of the beautiful woman tending him. Maybe she was a healer.

"You zigged when you should have zagged, and caught a hoof," the woman said.

Dominic frowned. Strange words. Nothing felt or sounded quite right.

"Actually, it was a glancing blow, and Bob Welch, our on-site paramedic, assures me there's no concussion or broken bones."

Beautiful or not, the woman's speech was peculiar, almost as if she were speaking a foreign language. Not to mention the fact that she talked as if he should know what a bobwelch was, or a pair of something.

Remi stared down into clear—no *startlingly* clear—blue eyes, feeling as if she had seen this man before. There was something vaguely familiar about him. In fact, now that she thought about it, he looked very much like the knight in the book . . .

"Oh, yeah, right," she said under her breath.

She was genuinely glad the man was okay, but now, after learning that he wasn't seriously hurt, she was also a hairbreadth away from reading him the riot act.

The man had nearly given her a coronary, getting smacked in the head like that. He upset the customers. Disrupted the whole show. What kind of weirdo, she wondered, puts on a costume, and jumps into the middle of a theatrical performance? At the moment, her greatest concern was making sure this joker didn't blame Swords and Shields for what happened, and run screaming for his lawyers. Remi stood up, and smiled. "So, how's the head feel now?"

On his second try, Dominic succeeded in raising himself onto one elbow. This time his head throbbed less. He looked up at the woman, and nodded.

"Good." She propped her hands at her waist, and her smile abruptly disappeared. "Then perhaps you can tell me just what the hell you thought you were doing out there tonight?"

Dominic stared at her, shocked at such blasphemous language coming from a gentlewoman.

"You could have gotten yourself killed. You know that, don't you?"

He blinked, wondering if she was demented. Of course he could have been killed. Men died in battle. What was honor worth, if not a man's life?

"Don't blink those baby blues at me, Mr. . . . ." Remi paused, expecting him to respond appropriately. When he didn't, her frustration elevated. "What's your name?" she said with great deliberation.

"Who—who *are* you?" Dominic managed to ask at last.

"Finally—" she threw her hands in the air "—he speaks. And no fair. I asked you first."

When he didn't respond, Remi's frustration rose like the mercury in a thermometer on a July day. "Am I supposed to torture you to get your name? Is it some big secret?"

*Torture!*

Dominic's rapidly clearing mind latched on to the word like a snapping turtle. Had his men surrendered while he lay unconscious? Was he Richard's prisoner? But this was no dungeon. Nor were there any guards present. And how could a mere woman hope to torture a seasoned knight?

"Look, Mr. Whatever-your-name-is." Remi moved away from the bed. "All I want is some simple information so I can decide what to do with you." As she stepped away, the gold stars and half moons imprinted on the sapphire blue fabric of her costume caught the light.

Unexpectedly, Dominic was struck by the woman's grace and beauty, and by the richness of her gown. The fabric was costly—probably satin—and embroidered with gold. Only a noblewoman could afford such clothes. Or a wealthy man's leman. With all the riches of a kingdom at his command, Richard the Third was certainly a very wealthy man. Despite his small stature, and homely face, it was rumored Richard had exquisite taste when it came to his paramours.

It was also whispered that he consorted with magicians and sorcerers, and that many members of his court, especially his lovers, dabbled in the black arts. Was it possible this woman was a witch in Richard's employ?

And who would know better than he about how witchery and black magic could appear normal? Instinctively, his thumb worried the ring on the little finger of his right hand. When his mother, Alise, had given it to him, she had insisted that he never be without it. And he never had, only moving it to a different finger as his hand grew. She had told him the ring was magic and that someday he would know its true meaning.

Had he not lived his entire life with his own mother under suspicion of witchcraft? Truth be told, hadn't he even suspected it himself a time or two?

If this woman was a sorceress, it would explain the strange voice he heard before he fell unconscious. It would also explain why everything around him felt familiar, yet . . . unnatural.

"So what's it gonna be?" Remi said. "Do you tell me what I want to know, or do I call the authorities?" As she spoke, Remi took a couple of steps toward the telephone positioned at one end of the counter.

When she moved, Dominic caught a glimpse of a small table behind where she had been standing. On the table, perched on a golden pedestal, rested a shining sphere, reflecting the light with a rainbow of colors. It was the same kind of ball he had seen in his mother's possession once many years ago.

A sorcerer's tool.

Dominic sat up on the side of the bed. For a second, his head swam, then cleared. "What is that?" He pointed to the sphere.

Remi glanced over her shoulder. "A crystal ball. What's it look like?"

"And that?" He indicated the wand beside the ball.

She turned back to face him. "A magic wand."

"And they... they belong to you?"

"Yes, they belong to me," she answered, irritated at the guy's refusal to explain his behavior or even give his name. She went back to the table. "And at the moment, I wish my crystal ball wasn't bogus, and that I had..." She picked up the wand, and tapped it against her palm several times. The light flickered, then disappeared. "New batteries for this damned thing. Then maybe I could find out something about you." Remi looked up to find the impromptu knight staring at the wand as if he had just seen a live cobra.

Dominic's focus ricocheted from the wand to the room, this time seeing it from a new point of view. The bottle and jars in the cupboards. Did they contain secret potions and poisons? The candles. Their flames did not waver, and no wax dripped. Was that because they were part of the witch's magic? The walls, the floor, the bed. All made to look real to fool him? To trap him? Was any of what he saw real? Had she cast a spell on him? His gaze went to the woman.

Sorceress!

He had to escape.

When he continued to stare, Remi stared right back. "What's your problem?"

"I fear, mistress, that you—" Dominic stood up, swaying on his feet "—are my problem."

Remi rushed to his side, slipping a supporting arm around his waist. "Oh, no, you don't. I'm not going to have you keel over, and wind up with another goose-egg-size knot on your head."

Whoa, Remi thought. This guy was a real hardbody. Even through the leather, she could feel the power of well-honed muscles. She glanced up, for the first time really looking at her charge. And not too shabby in the looks department, either, she decided. The strength in his jawline alone would be enough to make most women's heartbeats jump like a triphammer.

No daydream here. The power in his face and body definitely reminded her of the picture of the knight in the book Mark had sent her. Not shabby at all. Just her luck. A knight in shining armor finally shows up, and he's been jousting without a helmet. She might be frustrated, but that didn't mean she couldn't appreciate a well-put-together male when she saw one, her inexperience notwithstanding.

Dominic glanced down at the woman he suspected was in league with the devil. But when his gaze met hers, demons were the last things on his mind. Suddenly, he could not remember encountering a woman of such uncommon beauty. In fact, at the moment, he could not recall one single woman he had been with or even thought of, in many years.

Her skin looked as soft as rose petals, her green eyes sparkled with the kind of fire he had only seen in exquisite emeralds, and she smelled of lilacs in spring. Her hair, long and unbound, tumbled over her shoulders in tempting disarray. Wildly curly, its honey-blond color danced with golden lights. And her body felt so ripe and warm against his. In truth, the woman was enchanting; lovely beyond any he had seen in many a day.

Enchanting!

Of course she was enchanting. She was supposed to be. Did not Satan always use a man's lust as a weapon against himself?

In a move so startlingly fast it caught Remi totally off guard, the man yanked himself free. "Do you know who I am?"

Her eyes widened in astonishment. "Just what in Sam Hill do you think I've been—"

"I am Longmont, Knight of the Realm, and vassal to the Duke of Kerwick." The man drew himself up to his full and considerable height. "And you will get nothing from me. No amount of brutality or witchcraft will force me to betray my honor or the rightful king of England."

"The rightful . . . oh, now, wait a minute. This has gone far enough."

Over the witch's right shoulder—for Dominic was now almost certain he was dealing with black magic—he spied his armor, chain mail and sword. "It has indeed, mistress," he said, a plan of escape forming in his mind, a prayer forming in his heart. How powerful was she? he wondered, remembering stories from his youth about the horrible deaths some men had endured as the result of witchcraft. For a moment, fear overtook him, pushing away sanity. He prayed for strength to fight this evil.

Remi took a step toward him, and he jumped as if startled. Then he began to back away, moving around to her right. This guy was really spooked. For a second or two, she had seen the confusion and terror in his eyes. Could that horse have done more damage than she'd originally thought? Maybe she should get him to a hospital just to be sure.

At that thought, Remi's conscience pricked her. Understandably, the man was confused and afraid. Whether that condition began before or after he'd been hit on the head didn't really matter; the man needed help. Humor the guy, she decided. For all she knew, he could be one of those people who always wanted to join the circus, and this was as close as he could get. Or maybe he was an out-of-work actor. A very desperate out-of-work actor. Remi sighed, sympathy finally overriding irritation. "Is there someone I can call to come for you?"

"Call Satan himself, if you like." Dominic continued to circle around in order to reach his weapon.

Despite the fact that the guy sounded a little weird, she couldn't forget the look in his eyes a moment ago, and she couldn't shake the feeling that he was more lost than crazy. Maybe a bit bizarre, but not dangerous. Besides, until she could determine exactly who, and what he was, he *was* her responsibility. More specifically, the responsibility of Swords and Shields. The situation was delicate, to say the least, and she had to handle it just right or the company could be in for major attorneys' fees, and a big-time hassle. But then, she had a long history of dealing with the bizarre, so this should be a piece of cake.

"All right, Mr. Longmont—"

"Sir."

"Pardon?"

"Sir Longmont."

Remi shot him a questionable look, but smiled, and said, "Sure. Whatever you say."

"Release me."

"I beg your pardon?"

"I demand that you release me."

His attitude punctured a hole in the sympathy she'd felt a moment earlier. "I'm not holding you prisoner, Mr.—Sir Longmont. You're free to go, but I think—"

"You bring me here, then tell me I may go. What kind of witch's rhetoric is this? What evil have you planned?"

Another drop or two of sympathy disappeared. The witch thing was wearing thin. Hadn't his mother ever taught him it was rude to call people names? "Believe me, my only concern is to make sure you're okay."

"Liar."

The last of Remi's sympathy went up in smoke. "That's it." She threw up her hands, and headed for the phone. Loony-tunes or not, she'd had enough. "I don't care if you think you're the next Olivier. I don't even care if you're the best-looking fruitcake I've ever seen. Enough is enough. Now, I'm sorry you were hurt, and I understand you're upset. If you feel the need to go to the emergency room, I'll be happy to drive you, and, of course, Swords and Shields will pay for your treatment. But if this is your idea of a clever job interview, I'm sorry, but—"

"Cease your prattle, woman!"

"Cease my—" Remi turned, and found a sword inches from her heart.

She gasped, fear shooting through her body like a hot current through live wires. The blood in her veins tingled with an adrenaline rush. She held up a hand. Lord, the man really was loony-tunes.

"H-hold it, fella—Long—Longmont—Sir—whatever your name is." She took a deep, unsteady breath. "Don't get crazy on me."

Dominic gauged the distance from his position, wondering about the extent of her powers. Could she prevent him from reaching the door? Honor, indeed his sanity, gave him no choice but to escape, no matter the price.

"Believe me, lovely witch." Without taking his eyes from her face, he reached behind him, grasped his chain mail and draped part of it over the well-muscled arm holding the sword. The rest he held in his free hand. "I have no desire to bring down the wrath of your fellow wizards and warlocks on my head. I wish only to return to my men."

Remi swallowed hard. "That's cool."

"Where is Navarr?"

"Who?"

"What have you done with him?"

Oh, this guy was right on the edge. Remi licked her lips. "Him who?"

"None of your word tricks. What have you done with my war-horse?"

Remi was almost relieved to discover his request was relatively normal, if anything about this situation could be termed normal. "He's, uh, I, uh, think, I mean, he's probably with the rest of the horses." Just about the time she expected him to ask where, he nodded as if he knew.

Chain mail in hand, Dominic tested the door, and found it unlocked. His gaze met hers. "Another trick? What is waiting for me beyond this door?"

"A—a hall." Nothing remained of the fear she had seen earlier. In fact, the look in his eyes was as hard as cold steel. "I swear."

"Your oath means little." He had no way of knowing what evil she had conjured up to destroy him, but no matter. He would face it, and find some way to break free of her spell. As he had in countless battles in the past, Dominic drew on the well of inner strength that had always been his bulwark against fear.

As Remi's gaze met his, her eyes widened. Good grief, he really believed what he was saying. He actually thought he was a knight, and she was a witch. As bizarre as the idea was, Remi realized it was true, and she also realized that she couldn't let him run around loose in this condition. She took a step toward him. "Please—"

Dominic yanked open the door, and disappeared.

"No! Wait!" Without thinking, she ran after him.

Relying on instinct, Dominic hurried along a passageway he was certain led to the castle bailey. Once there, the stables, and Navarr, were not far away. Suddenly, behind him, he heard footsteps.

"God's teeth!" he hissed. "She comes for me."

"Please! Don't go," came the not-so-distant plea.

Her voice sounded so like the one that had first bewitched and beguiled him, so soft and compelling, that for a moment Dominic stopped.

Do not listen! reason demanded. He feared she wanted his soul. Sword in hand, he raced on, determined to break free of her spell or die. At last he saw a door ahead. He was only yards away from freedom, and the footsteps were coming closer, and closer.

"Wait!" he heard her call from right behind him. Dominic yanked open the door.

And stopped dead still.

"Thank goodness," Remi said, trying to catch her breath. She grabbed his arm when she reached him. "You can't go like this."

Chain mail slithered to the floor. He stood staring straight ahead as if he had turned to stone.

"Did you hear me?" Remi looked out into the humid August night, wondering what had brought him to a screeching halt.

The extensive Swords and Shields parking lot stretched out toward the service road of Stemmons Expressway, wet and empty except for her classic Mustang. Even at this late hour, traffic was steady. As cars zoomed along the eight-lane expressway, the tall halogen quartz lights occasionally caught a twinkle of chrome. The partially completed twenty-five-story office complex on the other side of the expressway was dark except for the occasional bolt of lightning, the obligatory lights on the roof to warn planes and the three generators hanging from cranes, secure for the night. Nothing unusual at all, as far as she could see.

Suddenly, the man lurched back inside, and slammed the door.

He leaned against the wall, his face drained of color, his breath coming in gasps. The sword that had been such a threat only moments ago hung loosely within his grasp and he looked ready to faint as his gaze met hers.

"Sorceress," he whispered, his voice shaking. "God save me."

# 3

"I'M NOT a sorceress. I only want to help you. Please—" Remi reached out a hand "—let me call a doctor."

Instinctively, Dominic backed away, then abruptly stopped. Trapped like a wild animal, his warrior's instincts overrode his fear and shock. Before Remi realized what was happening, he grabbed her hand, spun her around and yanked her hard against his chest . . .

And brought the razor-sharp edge of his sword to her throat.

"Free me from your spell, or I swear, you will be a headless witch." Dominic had no idea if his threat would succeed, but that did not deter him. The woman might have powers beyond his imagination, but he would not submit without a fight.

The sword rested lightly, but oh, so dangerously, at the hollow of Remi's slender neck, and his forearm was clamped so tightly across her midriff, only shallow breaths were possible. "I'm not . . . a witch."

He bent his head close to hers. "You lie. I beheld your devilry with my own eyes."

"Please, oh, please —"

"What? Do you beg for mercy?" Her feigned weakness was undoubtedly another trick.

"Yes. If that's w-what y-you want. Please, please," she whimpered, her voice again reminiscent of the one that had first bewitched him. "Don't hurt me."

Taken slightly aback by the haunting desperation in the woman's voice, Dominic had to remind himself that she was cunning and clever. Yet the fear in her voice was real, and beneath his forearm her heartbeat raced like wild horses.

How could this be? Why would a worker of the black arts fear a mortal?

Then he realized she had left her sorceress's tools behind in the antechamber. Was she helpless without them?

The thought renewed his hope, fortified his resolve. If he could keep her away from the crystal ball and wand, perhaps he had a chance. Glancing down the hallway, he saw a door. And if he could confine her, then he could find Navarr, and escape.

A small puff of air whooshed from Remi's lungs as her feet suddenly left the floor. Her heartbeat hammered against her chest, and the blood pounded at her temples so hard she felt light-headed.

Holding her tightly against his chest, Dominic carried her with him to the door. His forearm across her midriff provided a shelf for her breasts as they strained against her bodice and threatened to spill over their tenuous confinement. Despite his fear, despite his confusion, Dominic reacted to the sight of such tempting flesh.

"Give me the key," he growled, his breath hot on her cheek.

He was holding her so tightly, she barely managed to croak out the word, "Unlocked." Remi almost couldn't believe her eyes or her luck. They were standing in front of *her* office. Inside was a phone to call the security officer as well as a can of pepper spray. Inside was hope of freedom.

Dominic reached for the door handle, then paused, recalling the strange things he had seen through the other door. What if more of the same awaited him on the other side of this portal? Or worse? Whatever was on the other side, his captive would be the first to find out.

He slackened his hold on the woman enough for her body to slide down his until her feet touched the floor, but not enough for her to move, much less contemplate escape. "Hear me, enchantress. Do as I tell you or the first thing to enter this room will be your head."

He released her. The sword slid away from her throat, but a second later Remi felt the point between her shoulder blades. Dominic reached around her, and flung open the door.

The interior was so dark he could scarcely make out the familiar high stone walls of another antechamber. But it did not appear to be bewitched.

"Slowly," he ordered, urging her forward. "And remember, whatever fate you had planned for me, you will meet first."

On trembling legs, Remi took a halting step inside . . . and automatically flicked on the light switch.

"God's teeth!" Dominic hissed, staggering backward. Aiming for the door and escape, he misjudged his direction, and hit the cold stone wall.

Taking full advantage of her captor's momentary shock, Remi dashed across her office, jerked open her desk drawer and scooped up the cylinder of pepper spray that she had bought a year ago, and had never had occasion to use.

"Stay away from me," she warned, grasping the cylinder with both hands to minimize the fact that she was shaking. "Y-you just stay away from me."

Stunned, Dominic looked around the room, and realized that either he had died, and been sent forthwith to hell or this woman's powers were equal to those of Satan himself.

The room was filled with light, but he knew not its source. A painting of the witch wearing the same gown she wore now hung on the wall. But the artist must have been a warlock, because the likeness was so startlingly real he would not have been surprised to hear it speak. The furniture was odd-shaped: the table before her half of a circle of wood, and a chair with strange metal legs stood in the corner, the fabric of a color he had never seen before. And there was music. Music coming from . . . everywhere. And nowhere.

Had she robbed him of his sanity, and his soul?

Mindless or soulless, Dominic had no more questions about the extent of her power. It was more potent than he had ever imagined.

As a child, he had learned he had to fight, and fight hard, for everything he got in life. As an adult, he had learned there were more ways to fight than with a sword, and that in order to have the advantage, he must decide where, when and how to fight. As a warrior, he had learned that such decisions often must be made in the blink of an eye. This was such a moment.

Although his pride denied the idea of complete surrender, reality could not be ignored, and he faced the fact that he would do whatever was required of him in order to return to his men, to return to honor. For Dominic, his course was clear. He would flatter, cajole and make her feel she had won. He would lie— God forgive him—with a smile on his face if he had to.

He lay his sword on the floor, far enough away from him hopefully to give her a false sense of security, but close enough that he could reach it before she did, if need be.

"I offer you whatever boon you wish, enchantress. Whatever service you require, save betraying my king and country. I would die before swearing allegiance to Richard."

"Look, I don't know anybody named Richard. And I don't know if you're crazy or just plain stupid, but read my lips . . . I—am—not—a—witch."

"Sorceress, then. Enchantress. Whatever name you prefer. Simply tell me what I must do to be returned to the battle, and I will—"

"Battle? What *battle*, for crying out loud?" Between fear and frustration, Remi had just about reached the end of her rope.

"Why do you toy with me? You know full well the battle of which I speak. It rages now outside the very walls of the castle."

"The only battle going on around here is in your mind, fella." Remi picked up the phone, but found she was still shaking so hard she could barely dial the three-digit number to contact the security guard's station near the main entrance. With her other hand, she kept the can of pepper spray pointed in his direction.

"I'm calling security, so don't try anything."

Impatiently, Remi heard ring after unanswered ring at the other end of the line. "Damn!" She slammed down the receiver, realizing the guard was probably making his rounds. She racked her brain trying to recall his route through the building and the man's schedule. Double damn, she thought, remembering that he changed it every few days. The officer could be right down the hall or at the farthermost corner of the building now. The only thing she knew for certain was that sooner or later he *would* show up at her office door.

She had to stay cool. Remi took a deep breath. Help was on the way, and she was going be fine.

Calmer now, she looked at the maniacal knight, wondering if he could see that her bravado was little more than a bluff. All she had to do was make sure the situation didn't erupt again. All she had to do was stay cool, and everything would be fine.

Steadying his emotions, Dominic looked at the woman, wondering if she could see through his pretense of submission. All he had to do was convince her that he would do her bidding. All he had to do was form a plan of escape, and wait for the right moment to break free.

"I beg you," he said sincerely, "make known your boon so that I may attend to it forthwith. Time is of the essence if I hope to prevent the fall of Kerwick Castle. My men still fill the battlements, but I must lead—"

"Well, I'll give you one thing..." Remi had been only half listening to his ramblings until she heard him mention the name Kerwick. "You're good. You must have done a heck of a lot of research to find the name of this castle."

Dominic frowned. "How would I not know the name of my home...fair lady?" he asked, gentling his voice in hopes of appearing less threatening.

Remi noticed that he, too, had calmed considerably from a few moments ago. The stunned expression on his face was gone. In fact, he looked almost . . . normal. Whatever normal was for this broad-shouldered, steely-eyed pretender. Still, she reminded herself, a few moments ago, he *had* put a sword to her throat.

"Home?" she asked, carefully watching him.

"Aye. It has been so since I was a child."

"Kerwick Castle? This—" she pointed to the floor "—Kerwick Castle?"

"I know of no other."

Strange, Remi thought, that a man out to disrupt a performance would go to the trouble of uncovering the obscure name of a previously deserted castle that had been disassembled brick by brick in England, and reassembled in Texas. Only a handful of Swords and Shields executives knew the castle's actual name.

"You mean, it once belonged to your family?" Maybe this was the reason the guy had chosen this place to go bonkers.

There was a long pause before he replied, "Nay, not mine. I am only a vassal to the duke. Lady, please," Dominic urged, "my men are dying."

"In this battle you keep talking about?"

"Aye."

Remi had more than a working knowledge of dates and places in the medieval period. Having lived in England during her teens, she also had a good deal of firsthand knowledge.

"And exactly what battle would that be?"

Dominic eyed her closely. Why was she seeking what she must surely know? If this was some witch's trick, she would not find him such easy sport. "One of many fought to put Henry Tudor on the throne of England," Dominic replied, careful to play along until he could seize the opportunity to escape. "This day, we were part of a large force that was separated. Most of the men engaged the king's army at Bosworth or Redmore Plain. I know not how they fare, but—"

"Are you talking about Bosworth Field? In fourteen... She mentally rifled through her memory banks, searching for the correct year. "In 1485?"

"Aye, lady." At last, Dominic thought, she spoke with some reason, but to what purpose? More trickery?

This guy really has lost it, Remi decided. A smidgen of the sympathy she had experienced shortly after he regained consciousness resurrected itself, and her heart softened. She glanced at the digital clock on the CD player. He was either the greatest actor in the world, or he actually believed he was a fifteenth-century knight. Either way, she reminded herself, he wasn't stable. She hoped Wally or J.D., or whoever was working security tonight, hurried. This guy needed help. But until help arrived, Remi knew she needed to keep him calm.

"So, you were in the middle of the battle of Bosworth Field—"

"Nay. My men and I had taken a stand outside the castle against a small group of Richard's forces."

"That would be Richard the Third?"

"Aye." While Dominic wanted it to appear that he was cooperating, he was determined to give as little real information as possible.

"So, that means that you were fighting for, uh, Henry the Seventh?"

"He will be so named when he is crowned." Why was she asking questions for which she surely held the answers?

"Oh, he'll be crowned. Trust me."

A strange request coming from an ally of Richard's, Dominic thought, yet she sounded so positive. Regardless, trusting her was the last thing he intended to do. "That, of course, is the hope of many a loyal Englishman."

"Which you are."

"I would lay down my life for the rightful king," Dominic vowed quietly, his steely gaze drilling her.

Great. Not just a weirdo, but a committed weirdo. Remi glanced at the door, wondering how much longer it would be before the guard showed up.

"And I *must* return."

The desperation in his voice was so compelling, it took her off guard. Rarely had she been faced with such unadulterated assurance.

But he *couldn't* be who he claimed to be. It simply wasn't possible. Possible or not, Remi recognized fervor when she saw it, and this man *was* desperate to return to wherever he'd come from. He couldn't be gone soon enough to suit her.

Then an idea popped into her head. An idea so preposterously simple, Remi didn't know why she hadn't thought of it before. Probably because being threatened with a sword inhibits creativity.

It was too much to even hope for, but it would certainly save her wannabe knight a trip to jail, and her manager a lot of headaches, not to mention saving Swords and Shields a lot of negative publicity.

"Hey," she said, deciding she could probably talk all day and not put a dent in the kind of iron-willed determination she saw in his eyes, "don't let me stop you. I'm sure willing to forget all about this little . . . incident. Please, feel free to leave anytime."

Dominic almost couldn't believe his ears. She was setting him free! "And how can this happen?" he asked, glancing around for some mystical object he had not seen before. "Must we fetch your crystal ball and magic wand?"

"Excuse me?"

"Can you end the spell with only the magic words?"

"What words?"

"The ones you spoke to mesmerize me in the midst of battle. The ones spoken in the language of the devil."

"Language of the devil?" She rolled her eyes. "Give me a break."

"Aye. And after the words, you sent the mysterious lightning. The instant it struck my sword, my body shook, almost as if I could feel the lightning rushing through—"

"Through your blood," Remi finished for him. All of a sudden, the hair on the back of her neck raised as she remembered the sensations she had experienced when the lightning struck the arena floor tonight just before...

Just before the wrong knight came through the cloud of smoke.

A funny kind of smoke, at that, Remi thought, recalling the way the air had crackled and popped.

And then there was the unprogrammed lightning bolt.

Followed by a man dressed in the most realistic armor she had ever seen, acting like a real knight fighting for king and country.

Almost as if he'd stepped through some kind of time warp.

As soon as the words formed in Remi's mind, a totally bizarre idea began to form.

No, she warned herself, a little embarrassed that her imagination had taken such an absurd leap. What she was thinking was absurd. Totally absurd.

But she *was* thinking it. Thinking that perhaps— maybe, possibly—she was dealing with...

Time travel?

And the more she thought about it, the more momentum the idea gained. *Now* who was loony-tunes?

It was crazy, of course. People couldn't travel through time except in an H. G. Wells novel, right?

Absolutely.

Still, the idea persisted. In fact, took root—deep root. And as out-of-left-field as it sounded, her mind tracked the series of events like a bloodhound.

First the chants from the Druid book.

Then all that weird lightning and stuff. And all those weird vibrations.

Then her would-be knight arrived, continually getting in the way as if he'd never even been to a rehearsal. In the end, he got knocked out.

When he woke up, he thought she had jerked him out of a battle by using witchcraft. Then he went tearing out of the room, and freaked out when he got a glimpse of the parking lot. He freaked again when she turned on the lights.

The parking lot? What could have been so terrifying about the parking lot? Or lights? Why would he get so upset over cars zipping along the expressway and something as simple as electricity? You'd think the guy had been raised in a cave somewhere...

*Or a castle?*

No, she was losing her mind. He couldn't be a real knight. That would mean that... No way. This whole idea of time travel was too far off the deep end to even contemplate.

*But it would sure explain a lot of his weird behavior.*

Like his total shock and fear when she'd switched on the light.

*Like his absolute desperation to get back to comrades he was convinced were dying?*

Remi told herself she was undoubtedly slipping over the edge of madness. But it made sense. Bizarre sense, but sense, nonetheless. The question was, how did she prove this totally insane theory?

She looked at her pretender knight. Why was she even giving this man the benefit of the doubt, much less believing he was from another time?

The answer was in his eyes. There, in those clear blue depths was a certainty that had never wavered from the first moment they'd met. Even when he was frustrated, angry, and yes, even frightened, that certainty had remained. He knew who and what he was. There was no question. He was like an age-old rock cliff that stood against the sea. He knew his place and purpose. It was that confidence, that implicit conviction that gave credence to her theory and reason to an otherwise insane supposition.

"W-why did you s-stop when you opened the door to the . . . outside?" she stammered, her mind still warring between acceptance and the absurdity of her idea. "What did you see?"

"Magic," he said coldly.

"But, what did you *see?*"

"Witchcraft. Black magic. Call it by whatever name you wish," he said sardonically.

"Describe what you saw," she insisted.

"No."

"Why?"

"There is no need to speak again of such evil things."

"Did you see cars? The expressway?" He stared at her as if he had no idea what she was talking about. "Did you see anything familiar?"

"Lady," he practically bit out the word. "You know well I did not. Do you think me slow-witted?"

"No, unfortunately." Nervously, Remi licked her lips. "Okay. Let's take another tack. Do you know where you are now?" Abruptly, she waved her hand in front of her as if to erase the words. "Never mind. America wasn't even discovered for another seven years."

Remi looked at the man who could, if her theory was right, be a real live knight. Not one of her actors hired and trained to play a part, but an honest-to-God in-the-flesh medieval knight.

But such a thing defied logic. It was impossible. Wasn't it?

But what if, by some quirk of the cosmos, she had recited an ancient Druid chant that could transport a man through time? What if the chant, combined with her call for a fearless champion, had found its mark? What if she was looking at the results?

She wondered what her knight would think of her idea. He already thought she was a witch. Would he think she was an insane witch?

"What is your name?" she asked. "Besides Longmont, I mean."

"I am Sir Dominic William Longmont."

"And I'm Maria Remington Balfour, but you can call me Remi," she said, feeling a little ridiculous introducing herself. "Well, Dominic," she hurried on, "what I'm about to suggest to you is going to sound, well, to be perfectly honest, it's going to sound totally insane, but . . ." She took a deep breath. "I'm beginning to believe, that is, I think that maybe, possibly, you could have, uh . . . traveled through time."

There! She'd said it out loud, and the sky wasn't falling, and the lunatic police weren't knocking at the door.

"What do you think?" she asked when he made no response to her hypothesis. "Do you believe such a thing is possible?"

"If that is what you have done, lady. I believe it."

"Just like that?"

"It is well known that a witch's spell can change a man into an animal. If you have changed me from one time to another, then it is so."

Remi stared at him, a little stunned at his reaction. More accurately, his lack of it. "That's it? One minute you're in 1485, then presto chango, you're in 1996 and that's all you have to say?"

"What do you wish me to say? I know not of these things—" he looked around the room "—yet they are here, as I am here. This is not a dream. So, it must be real or a spell."

She couldn't believe that a concept that had been almost unacceptable to her, appeared to be so completely acceptable to him. Until she reminded herself that in his time, belief in witches, curses and magic potions was widespread. Even the nobility accepted such practices as common. No wonder the idea sounded reasonable to him.

"Some choice I've got," she mumbled. "Magic or time travel."

At that moment, the phone rang.

Startled, Dominic's gaze darted around the room to see what had produced the sound.

"Hey, don't panic," Remi told him, reaching for the receiver. "It's only the telephone." She picked up something from her desk and the ringing stopped. "See."

No doubt, another of her magic tools. His suspicions were confirmed when she began to speak to someone or something he could not see.

"Hello," she said, setting the pepper spray on her desk.

"Miz Balfour," said the male voice at the other end, "I noticed your car was still in the lot. Thought I better check to make sure you were okay."

"Thanks, J.D., I, uh . . ."

Here was the opportunity she'd been waiting for. One word—help—and the security guard would have the Dallas police swarming all over the Swords and Shields building in two minutes. One word was all it would take. Yet, as she looked into the eyes of her knight she hesitated.

He stood in front of her, strong, almost defiant. His body language and steely-blue gaze were intended to convey power, and issue a warning. But Remi ignored the warning, and looked past it to the man in-side. To a man confused and desperately trying to retain control in an out-of-control situation. A situation she had created. Thanks to her, he was out of place. Lost.

"I, uh, appreciate your checking in, J.D., but I'm fine."

"You working late?"

"Yeah, but I, uh, don't think I'll be much longer."

"Need me to walk you to your car?" the guard asked.

"No, thanks," she said, still looking into Dominic's gaze. "I have someone with me. Good night, J.D." Remi hung up the phone.

In that moment, she had made the decision to believe him. To believe what appeared to be so unbelievable. And in doing so, she was about to take a course of action that might prove to be wrong. Even dangerous. She was certain now that Dominic *had* traveled through time.

But not on his own.

Somehow, she and that silly little book of chants had called him from the past. As far-out as it sounded, she had brought a fifteenth-century knight to the twentieth century. Her whim to add some authenticity to the program had backfired, big time.

And now she was responsible for helping him get back.

# 4

REMI LET OUT A BREATH as she ran her hands through her hair, pulling the heavy mass of curls away from her face. "Sit down, Dominic. We need to talk."

"I will stand."

"You'll change your mind, trust me."

"Why do you insist that I trust you?"

"What?"

"You asked me to trust you once before. Do you believe I would be so foolish? You speak to invisible spirits and most certainly are in league with the devil."

"Invisible spirits?" She stared at him for a second before it dawned on her what he meant. "Oh, the telephone. It's how we talk to each other. There's practically a phone on every corner. And I'm not actually asking you to trust me. Well, I am, but . . . It's an expression. You know, like 'no way,' or, um, 'get real,' or . . ." From the look of confusion on his face, Remi realized it must sound as if she was talking gibberish. She shook her head. "Oh, never mind."

When she sat down in the chair behind the desk, Dominic was surprised to see it turn and tilt. How many more strange things would he behold before he was safely back home? How many more spells did his beautiful captor have up her sleeve?

"These shoes may look like they're fit for a princess," Remi said, removing both of her soft leather slippers, "but they're killing my feet." She sighed, and wiggled her toes, then rubbed her tired feet over the plush carpet. All of which felt good—and was designed to delay the moment of telling him where he was, and that she had no idea how he got here, much less any idea of how to get him back.

He stood on the other side of the desk, unmoving, his gaze unwavering, waiting.

"Dominic—you don't mind if I call you by your first name, do you? The sir thing is kinda formal— I, uh, I know you want to uh, go back—"

"I must return to my men."

"Yes, well. You see, there's only one little problem." She tried to meet his gaze directly, but she couldn't. "I don't know how to get you back. In fact, I'm not really sure how you got here in the first place, although I—"

"But your power is strong."

"I don't have any *power!* Now listen to me very carefully," she insisted vehemently, waving a shoe in his direction. "I am not a witch or a sorceress. This is the twentieth century. Got it? It's five hundred years after you were born, and a whole helluva lot of things have changed. All that stuff you saw when you opened the door was real. Everybody drives a car. You can get pills at the corner drugstore to cure almost anything. We've got MTV, for crying out loud, and—"

Remi stopped. She was doing it again. He didn't, *couldn't* understand what she was saying. There was no way she could convince him that she had no magical powers. Every idea or tool that came to mind would only look like more magic to him.

"I take it back. You *are* going to have to trust me." Remi reached down, opened her bottom desk drawer and pulled out a pair of tennis shoes. "Yeah, right," she said under her breath as she slipped on the shoes and tied the laces. "When pigs fly."

"Your pardon, lady?"

"Nothing. Never mind," she said, standing.

"Are you saying you will not undo the spell?"

"I'm saying I don't know how."

"But that is not possible."

"You see there was this book of chants."

"Use it." She was playing with him. She knew the urgent need for him to return to his men, yet she prattled on. Frustrated and anxious, he wished there was some way to force her to do as he wanted.

"I don't remember which one I read."

From the way the muscles in his neck corded and his eyes darkened, Remi could see he thought her defense was lame.

"And we can't start reading every chant to find the right one. Lord knows what we might conjure up. Or blow up. Playing around with this stuff could be dangerous."

"But you brought me here. You are—"

"Responsible. I know, I know. And I'm not about to leave you in the lurch."

"God's blood! Will you speak English, mistress?" he demanded.

"I am. You're not listening," Remi insisted.

She put a hand on her hip, and took a deep breath. "Dominic," she said, her tone calmer, softer. "From this point on, you really are going to have to trust me. Everything you're going to see and hear will be strange, maybe even frightening. I'll do my best to explain things, but don't flip out if I forget and leave you in the dust."

"Beginning with this language you speak?" he said, the slightest edge of irritation in his voice.

"Yeah," Remi replied, slinging back a little attitude herself. Didn't the jerk realize she was trying to help him? "I'll try to watch my slang and vernacular, but you need to understand I can't stop every five minutes to give you a lesson in—"

"And you—" Dominic leaned forward and put his hands on her desk "—need to understand that I am not accustomed to being ordered about by a woman, even if she is a—"

"Don't say it." Remi held up her hand.

"Lady—" he straightened, giving her a look hard enough to cut steel "—you try my patience."

"Yeah, well, you'd be easier to take in small doses." She took a deep breath, and mentally counted to ten. "Look, snapping at each other isn't going to get us anywhere. It's late, we're both more than a little frazzled and we've got to figure out how to send you back. Agreed?"

"Aye." Dominic didn't like having to depend on her, but it couldn't be helped. He would agree with the devil himself if it would help him get to his men.

"Okay," she said. "The first thing we have to do is find someplace for you to stay."

"But the battle rages now—"

"I know, but, uh..." Remi realized he was in no mood for a lengthy conversation about the ins and outs of time travel, and she had to come up with a suitable explanation that would keep him calm until she could figure out what, if anything, to do. "It doesn't make any difference. Time is passing here, but when you go back, it will be the same as when you left," she insisted, hoping the concept of double talk originated some time after the fifteenth century.

"Are you certain?"

"That's the theory. And it should hold. In any case, we have to be certain about the chant. The wrong one could be disastrous."

He pondered the last statement for a moment before answering, "Very well, mistress. I will do as you say. There seems to be no other choice."

"Smart move. And since I got you into this mess, the least I can do is put you up in my condo." She eyed his tall, lean frame. "I'm not sure you'll fit on my couch, but it'll have to do temporarily."

"How will we travel to this condo place?"

"My car is in the parking lot."

"Car?"

"You'll see, but before we leave—"

"What about Navarr? I wish to make certain he is stabled."

"Well—" She thought for a moment. "I guess we can take a detour though the stables before we leave. Okay?"

"I am most grateful, my lady."

"Now," she said, attempting to grasp the zipper in the back of the dress. "I've got to get out of this costume." Remi stretched, but couldn't reach it. "Uh-oh."

"What does that mean?"

"It means, between you getting bonked on the head, and all the rushing around, I didn't change when Belva was here to help me, and it's—" she stretched again, straining to reach the zipper "—almost impossible to get out of this by myself. Could you just help me?"

"You want me to take your clothes off?"

Remi's head snapped up, her gaze meeting his.

It was a question, a statement and an invitation, all at the same time. The question was in the words, the statement in his tone of voice. Both of which she could understand and handle. The invitation was in his eyes, and sent sparks of awareness skipping through her body like water dancing on a hot griddle.

"No, uh, what I mean is that I need you to, uh..." He was staring at her breasts, and Remi was finding it extremely difficult to hang on to her train of thought. "... unzip me."

"Uh...?"

"Zip."

"Zip," he repeated, almost as if he were tasting the word.

His mouth was strong, like the man, the outline of his lips clearly defined. Yet they looked soft enough to coax a woman to surrender.

"Yes, well," she said, composing herself. She walked straight up to him and turned her back, lifting the heavy mass of hair from her neck. "All you have to do is find the little metal tab and pull it down."

Dominic stared at the smooth skin of her back. It looked as soft as silk, creamy and tempting. One stray curl had escaped her hold, and lay temptingly against her neck. Without thinking, he reached out to touch . . .

"See it?"

"What?" Quickly, he found the tab. "Aye, I have it."

"Okay, now just take hold, and pull it down."

Dominic did as she instructed, and a heartbeat later his eyes widened. As he pulled, the bodice sprang open, exposing more and more of her back, eventually leaving her bare to the waist.

"Thanks." Holding the unzipped bodice pressed to her breasts, she pivoted to face him. "Now, I'm going in that room there." She pointed toward the bathroom. "Promise me you won't try to leave again?"

"As loath as I am to admit it, mistress, you are my only hope of returning to my proper place. I will await you."

"Promise?"

"I never lie. Nor take unfair advantage, especially of a woman. My word is my honor, and I have given you my word."

"Good," Remi said. Just the same, once inside the bathroom, she was careful to leave the door ajar just the tiniest little bit in order to hear him if he tried to leave.

Dominic moved closer to the door, acutely aware of the sounds of fabric rustling. Acutely aware that a woman, a very beautiful woman, was disrobing only a few feet away. He could easily imagine the costly smooth satin gliding over her even smoother skin. The image did little to lessen his frustration.

In different circumstances, he might have been inclined to make the most of such an advantageous situation. Once again, he reminded himself that the woman in question, not he, had the advantage. She, and she alone, held the key to his future.

He saw the door move, and stepped back to his previous position. When she walked back into the room, Dominic could do nothing but stare at her like a bumbling youth.

"Much more comfortable, not to mention cooler," Remi announced, having changed into a T-shirt and a pair of shorts. Remi held up her two birthday gifts. "We need to take this with us." She kept the Druid volume and put *Rogues Across Time* on her desk. "And your armor, too. I'm sure it'll fit in the trunk of my... What now?" she asked, noticing his open mouth and stunned expression.

"Your—your legs. They are bare."

"Oh, sorry. I should have prepared you. That dress was a costume. You know, like in a play. There were plays in your time, right?"

"Aye, but—"

"I know it must look a little weird, but it's perfectly acceptable. In fact, a lot of people wear stuff like this in the summer, especially in Texas. Does it—" he just kept looking at her legs "—offend you?"

Regardless of the times, he was still a man. A normal, healthy, responsive man. He would hardly term the sight of her long, shapely bare legs offensive. Erotic, but not offensive. Seeing her exposed limbs made him wonder what they would feel like sliding over his own bare legs or wrapped around his waist.

"I . . ." He shook his head, hoping his body didn't betray him.

Remi smiled, stuffing the book into her purse and slinging it over her shoulder. "Good. Then let's collect your armor, say nightie-night to your horse and get out of here." She picked up the copy of *Rogues Across Time*, dropped the book into an open desk drawer, then pushed it closed.

They found his war-horse in the last stall. Dominic set down his armor and immediately went to Navarr.

"So, my friend." He stroked the stallion's neck. "You have fared well," he said, noticing that the horse had been groomed and fed. Blowing and snorting, Navarr jerked his head back as if to insert his own addendum to the statement.

"Yes. It is confusing, but we will be home soon. You will lead the charge as before, powerful as always." Listening to Dominic's soothing voice, the animal quieted. "Rest well," he told the horse, then picked up his armor.

Remi walked to the stable entrance, and using one of the house phones, called the security guard to let him know they were leaving.

Dominic followed her, still feeling as if he were in the middle of a dream. Moments later, he found himself standing in front of the same door he had opened earlier. The door to the magic that had frightened him the way no battle ever had.

Remi reached for the doorknob, then stopped. "You're not going to freak out on me again, are you?"

"Freak?"

"When I open this door, you're going to see all the things you saw before, so don't panic, all right?"

"You mean, the lights, and the...the other things."

"Yes. And there will be more *things*," she said, wondering what his reaction would be when she cranked up her Mustang "witchmobile," and went tearing off into the night. "You're just going to have to—"

"I know." He held up a hand. "Trust you."

"You got it. Ready?" His expression was unreadable in the half shadow of the security light over the door, but he hefted his armor higher in his arms.

"Aye."

Remi opened the door to the twentieth century, and he followed her through it.

"You okay?" she asked when he jumped at the sound of the heavy door closing.

He nodded, then glanced around, filling his lungs with the sultry night air. "It is real," he said with a touch of wonder.

"Yeah, sometimes too real." Remi understood that he expected it to be otherwise. Lord knew, she had wished it herself on occasion.

Dominic looked at her. "And what now?"

She couldn't help grinning, knowing the next twenty minutes were probably going to blow his mind. Pointing to her Mustang as she started walking toward it, Remi said, "C'mon. You're about to get the ride of your life."

Five minutes later, she wasn't sure they would ever leave the parking lot. Dominic had balked at the idea of climbing inside the "box of armor," and only her cross-my-heart-and-hope-to-die vow that he wouldn't be trapped had persuaded him to get in.

"Okay, now it's your turn," she instructed after having just demonstrated the not-so-graceful art of entering and exiting the small car. "Just bend your knees a little, and sort of dip and lean . . . and be careful not to—"

Too late. He banged his head on the Mustang's roof. "How can you tolerate such a confining space?" Dominic asked, rubbing the newly tender spot on his skull.

"Because it's a cool car." Remi replied, walking around to her side. She got in, slid under the steering wheel, closed her door and turned toward him. "Buckle up."

"Your pardon?" he asked, struggling to fold his long legs into a comfortable position.

"You have to—" she stretched her upper body across his chest, pushed down the button to lock his door, then grasped the safety harness and made the near-fatal mistake of looking up into his eyes "—buckle up."

They were breasts to chest, their faces close, their lips mere inches apart.

Instantly, Remi's heart was beating so fast it sounded like an orchestra of kettledrums in her ears. And the air in her lungs seemed to be in such ridiculously short supply, she had trouble catching her breath. Those eyes, she thought, would make Paul Newman green with envy. And his mouth—her gaze was drawn there. Oh, his mouth . . .

He shifted in his seat, causing Remi to snap out of her sensual trance. "It's, uh, a state law." She straightened, pulling the strap across his broad, hard-muscled chest, down past his waist and hip, dangerously close to his . . .

"There." She shoved the buckle into the latch, and jerked her hand—her none-too-steady hand—away. Fast. Gracious but her voice was breathy. "The last thing we need is a cop stopping us." Remi smiled, hoping she sounded more confident than she felt, and thanking her lucky stars policemen didn't issue tickets for lewd thoughts the way they did for lewd behavior, or she would be in big trouble.

She started the engine, glancing over at Dominic. "Okay?"

He nodded, not because he was afraid, but because, after having her body next to his, he wasn't sure she hadn't robbed him of the power of speech. Even through his leather tunic, the feel of her breasts pressed against him had brought a quick and undeniable reaction. She had been so close, so tempting that he had instinctively leaned into her, and almost put his hands on her before he realized his mistake. Thank the Lord she had pulled away when she did, and that the darkness helped cover the fact that his manhood strained painfully against his breeches. He still had not recovered from the way she was dressed, or rather, *un*dressed. The last few minutes hadn't helped cool his blood.

How could he be thinking such lustful thoughts when so much was at stake? How could the desires of the flesh ever make him forget his honor to his king, his country? They could not, he reminded himself.

But if Dominic had thought he was uncomfortable with Remi draped across his chest, that discomfort vanished the moment the car moved. His hands shot out to grasp the dashboard.

"Take it easy," she warned. "I'll get you there in one piece."

After several moments passed and he decided she might be telling the truth, a conveyance, similar to the one they were in, passed them. "Is that another witch?" Dominic asked, glancing over his shoulder, watching it speed out of sight.

"Nope. Probably just another poor slob like me, working late."

He was on the verge of telling her not to waste her time crying poverty because he had seen her costly garments, when another car flew by. Then another, and another. Soon they were in the midst of dozens of cars!

Remi watched his glance dart from one vehicle to the other, eyeing the drivers. "I told you," she said. "Everyone drives a car. This is the way everyone in my time gets from one place to another. There's no magic. We have huge buildings filled with . . ." She struggled for a way to explain machines and gave up, ". . . people who make these cars, then send them to merchants who sell them."

They pulled up to a stoplight. Dominic continued to check out the other cars, and Remi could see that he was struggling to process everything. The light changed, and they moved on, through a residential section, past several strip malls, apartments and a twenty-four-hour discount store with a near-full parking lot and busy shoppers, many of whom were wearing shorts and T-shirts of varying descriptions.

At the next stoplight, she glanced at him, and saw the first glimmer of comprehension in his expression.

The first real indication that he was at least beginning to grasp the fact that she was no different than anyone else in her time. That she had told him the truth.

"This is not magic."

It was a statement, not a question, and she breathed a small sigh of relief. But there was no relief in Dominic's eyes, only concern. She knew what was going through his mind.

If there was no magic, and she was just an ordinary person, could she send him back?

"Dominic, I'm going to do everything I know to help you return to your own time. I promise."

His gaze met hers, and he believed her. He could not say why he believed her, but he did. There was something innately honest about this woman, despite the freakish circumstances of their meeting.

"You have my undying gratitude, mistress."

"Could we lose the titles? Just Remi will do."

"Remi," he repeated, revising his earlier opinion that it sounded strange. Strange or not, it fit her perfectly.

He was quiet for the remainder of the drive to her condo, and Remi didn't attempt conversation. The poor guy was doing the best he could to handle this bizarre situation without her yapping about electricity and tollbooths. Besides, she had been right when she'd told him he would have to trust her for some things. In the end, he would have to find some way to cope with the twentieth century and all its oddities.

No explanation could accomplish that. That acceptance, that peace, would have to come from within Dominic.

"MAKE YOURSELF at home," Remi said as he followed her inside the condo. She closed the door, tossed her keys onto the narrow Egyptian table in the entryway then strolled through the living room headed for the kitchen. "I'm starving. How about you?"

She disappeared, then reappeared a second later, a plum in her hand. "Don't be intimidated by all the junk," she said, taking a bite of the fruit. "My taste in decorating runs to eclectic clutter, but it's comfortable. What are you doing?"

He was looking, staring, actually, at the wall of solid bookcases jam-packed with books.

"These all belong to you?"

She shrugged. "I'm a word junkie."

Her taste in reading, like her taste in decorating, was eclectic, including the clutter. The shelves contained everything from a rare first-edition Dickens, to current paperback romances. Mixed in with those, and in no apparent order except by a system known only to Remi, were volumes of *The Origins of Man*, *Grimm's Fairy Tales*, Shakespeare's and Sir Arthur Conan Doyle's complete works, histories of Egypt, Russia and the British Empire, and a copy of *Jaws*.

"You call yourself poor, but only great wealth could provide so many books."

"I'm not exactly destitute. Oh, you mean the 'poor slob' thing. I wasn't referring to my financial—"

"You have read them all?"

"Each and every one. Some more than once. That's one of the pluses, uh, joys of today, Dominic. Every city in this land has a library that anyone can enjoy, free."

He whipped around to face her. "Every city?"

"Yep. And if you want to own your books, they are priced so that anyone can buy them."

"Truly?" He turned back to stare at the hundreds of volumes.

"Truly. Mine have been all over the world with me. They're like my family."

Stunned to see so much knowledge amassed in one place, Dominic couldn't take his eyes off the books. Knighthood was his vocation, but his passion was learning. From infancy, his mother had instilled in him the fact that knowledge was power, that a learned man was a secure man. She had been his teacher as well as his parent, and the more she had taught him, the more he had wanted to learn. Now, to see so much information, so accessible, was almost incomprehensible. And wonderful.

Remi watched him. He was obviously impressed with her library. Knowing only the nobility and a select few had been taught to read in his time, his awe was understandable. If Dominic was one of those fortunate ones, his brief stay in the future would be considerably easier. On both of them. Behind her back, she crossed her fingers.

"Do you—"

"You said Richard was defeated. This one." He reached up to the top shelf for *Great Battles of England*, opened it and began flipping through the pages. "Does it contain an account of the battle?"

*At least I don't have to look for my copy of McGuffy's Reader.* "Probably. Taking thrones was big stuff back in those days. Still is, come to think of it."

The flipping ceased, and he ran his hand over the page before him. "'Lancaster and York—The Battle of Bosworth Field.'" His fingers glided over the words. Then they stilled.

"'Richard's deformities may have been exaggerated'" he read, "'but hardly his crimes. The crown was too tempting. There appears to be no doubt that Edward the Fifth and his young brother were murdered—'"

"Dominic." She stepped forward to take the book. "I don't think you should—"

"No." He held up his hand. "I want to know.

"'There appears to be no doubt that Edward the Fifth and his young brother were murdered in the Tower, and that Richard the Third was responsible for the deed. The bones—'"

Remi snatched the book away. "Don't read any more."

"He killed them," Dominic whispered, his hands balling into fists. "His own nephews, and he killed them."

"Or had them killed."

"There is no difference." His eyes flashed rage.

"No, of course not. He was a horrible man, but he's dead."

"I hope he is rotting in hell."

"I'd say that was a safe bet."

"My men? Is there an account of what happened to my men?"

Remi scanned the rest of the page and several after it. "There's no mention of Kerwick Castle or another battle. But this isn't the only work on the Wars of the Roses."

When he frowned, she explained, "So called because the white rose was the symbol of the House of York, and the red rose the symbol of the House of Lancaster. Bosworth Field was the last battle, and then the Tudors came to the throne. It pretty much heralded the end of the feudal system and the medieval era."

"If this book does not tell if my men lived or died…"

Their gazes met, and Remi could see the rest of the question in his eyes. The question she didn't want him to ask, but knew he must.

"Or if I lived or died?"

She didn't want to think about the possibility that he died in that battle. She didn't want to think that she might have to send him back to his death.

"You lived. You're alive and breathing."

"Here, but what about in my time?"

"Single-minded, aren't you?"

"I must know."

"Okay, okay, but not tonight. Tomorrow is Sunday and I give you my solemn promise that I will spend the whole day trying to find out what happened to everybody. Then we'll go over the chants with a fine-tooth comb and get some high-tech help."

"On the sabbath?"

"The on ramp to the information superhighway is never closed."

"Supper—"

"Super, and I'll explain it all to you in the morning." She closed the book and raised onto the tip of her toes to put it back on the shelf. "What do you say, we sleep on it?"

"Together?"

The unexpected question unnerved Remi so much, she almost lost her balance and dropped the book. "No," she assured him when she was once again steady on her feet. "That's not . . . we can't . . ." When had he moved closer to her? And why had she suddenly forgotten what she was going to say? Irritated at herself for being so flustered, Remi put her hands on her hips, and in her best assistant-manager voice informed him, "You get the futon."

# 5

THE FUTON, Dominic soon discovered when he tested it, was amazingly comfortable for such an odd-looking piece of furniture. Remi had brought out some colorful pieces of fabric that she explained were to be used for bed linens, and in no time his bed was ready. Then she bid him a polite but brief good-night and left the room.

He glanced down at the bed as he began removing his clothes. The last time he had prepared to sleep was hours before the battle. Had that only been one night past? It felt like years.

If it were not for fear that Remi would hear him and think him demented, Dominic would have laughed out loud. In one sense, it had been years since he'd slept. He had awakened in one time, and he would seek slumber in another.

Had he gone mad between sunrise and sunset?

Was everything he had seen and heard this day the ravings of his own lunatic mind? Perhaps it would be easier if that were true, but Dominic knew it was not. He was sane. Too sane perhaps. How did he reconcile this reality with his honor, an honor that refused to allow him to abandon his men? Yet he had no choice but to reconcile honor with this reality because he had so little control over the situation. Whether by Remi's hand or some bizarre twist of fate, he was in the future. A future both disquieting and fascinating.

*Remi.*

The woman was as fascinating as the time she lived in. Earlier, it had come as something of a shock for him to realize that his virility unsettled her. She had actually blushed when he'd asked if they were to sleep together. Dominic smiled to himself as he tossed the remainder of his garments over a nearby chair. She was a curious mixture of beauty, intelligence and almost virginal charm. He wondered how she would have reacted if he had touched her when they were in her car.

He had wanted to do more than touch.

"I thought since you weren't used to air-conditioning," Remi said, sailing back into the room carrying a blanket, "that you might like...ohmygod."

He was naked. Stark, staring naked.

The blanket hit the floor with a soft thud, and Remi spun around so fast the motion made a whooshing sound. "I didn't— I'm sorry. I never thought . . . oh, I'm so sorry."

"Is something amiss?"

"You, you, uh, don't have any clothes on."

"Aye."

"Well, uh, in this time, it's, uh, not customary to go around naked."

"Do you sleep in your clothes?"

"Sleep? No. Yes. In a way. Women usually wear gowns or pajamas, and men wear, well, actually, I'm not sure what men wear to bed since I don't make it a habit to . . . Never mind, just don't walk around that way, okay?"

"If that is your wish."

"It is. It most definitely is," she said, resisting a heavy-duty urge to glance over her shoulder as she bent down, reached behind her and retrieved the blanket. With an underhand pitch, she sent it flying toward him. "Tomorrow we'll have to see about getting you something to wear. G-good night, Dominic."

He caught the blanket in one hand. "Good night, my lady," he replied, but she had already left the room.

There it was again. That blend of strength and innocence he had noted before. One minute she was in charge of the situation, the next she was as shy as a maiden. Were all women in this century as complex as Remi?

It was one of the hundreds of unanswered questions crowding his mind. Surely, he thought, gazing at the magnificent library, with so much knowledge at her fingertips, Remi would be able to help him. He stretched out on the futon and covered himself with the colorful fabric. He could do nothing tonight. Tomorrow would bring answers. Tomorrow would see him back where he belonged.

REMI MADE a hasty retreat to her office.

"I've got to get him back to where he belongs," she mumbled, switching on her computer. "Got to. He's ... he's ..."

*Naked in my living room!*

"Oh, get a grip," she told the menu that had just popped up on the monitor. "You've seen naked men before."

*Not like that.*

It was true. She'd only gotten a glimpse of Dominic, but that was enough.

He took her breath away.

His body was lean and hard, with muscles so beautifully defined he could have modeled for Michelangelo. But he wasn't buffed and pretty like a modern bodybuilder. There were scars. She'd glimpsed one on his right shoulder. Because the scar was so obvious, it was reasonable to assume the wound that had caused it must have been painful. Maybe even life-threatening?

Why the thought of him in pain, possibly near death, should suddenly bring tears to her eyes, she couldn't fathom, but it did. "Don't be ridiculous," she sniffed. "He's a warrior. And warriors get hurt or killed ..."

Is that what had happened to Dominic in his time? And if she found a way to send him back, was she sending him to his death?

Remi shook her head as if she could dislodge the disturbing thoughts, and concentrated on calling up her provider service. She needed information if she was going to help Dominic, and she needed it pronto.

While he slept, Remi surfed the Internet, requesting, gathering any and every fact she could on the battle of Bosworth Field and Sir Dominic William Longmont. Information on the battle kept her fax machine humming, but there was nothing regarding Dominic. Finally, after exhausting her meager talents in cyberspace, she settled for enlisting the aid of an information broker. Hopefully, tomorrow would bring answers.

DOMINIC AWOKE to a tantalizing aroma. For a split second, he was startled, until he remembered the events of the night before. And Remi.

He was in her—what had she called it?—a condo. Strange name, but then, so much of what he had seen had strange names. One thing was recognizable. Whatever the unknown but mouth-watering smell was, it was food, and he was ravenous.

Dominic rose from his bed, determined to find the source of the aroma. He had taken several steps toward the hallway, when he remembered Remi's reaction to his nakedness. He grabbed the sheet and wrapped it around himself, sufficient to cover what needed to be covered. Then he simply followed his nose to the kitchen.

"Good morning, mistress."

Remi jumped at the sound of his voice, and turned toward him, her hand over her racing heart. "Good grief, you scared me half to death."

"It was probably the sound of my rumbling belly that frightened you."

Her gaze drifted from his face, over his bare chest, to where his hand rested on his stomach just above the sheet knotted at his waist. She yanked her gaze back to his face.

"I must speak of a most delicate matter," he said.

"Delicate?"

"Your privy, mistress?"

"What? Oh, that. Yeah, uh, well, it's right down the hall."

When he looked dubious, she realized she would have to show him. "Follow me," she said and led him to the bathroom. "Okay, now you, uh, you know, relieve yourself, there." She pointed to the toilet. "And when you're done, you just push this handle down..."

Her demonstration of flushing startled him and he stepped back.

"I'll be in the kitchen when you, uh, finish." Remi beat a hasty retreat. "No one would believe this," she mumbled, going to the pantry for some waffle mix.

"I thought I might have dreamed last night," he said when he joined her a few moments later. "But obviously this is no dream."

"No, it's not."

"Might I inquire if you know any more about our... situation?"

She shook her head. "I'm sorry. But don't let it get you down, okay. I'll find a way. I promised, remember?"

"Aye."

"Would you like some coffee?"

"Perhaps. Pray tell, what is it?"

"A drink. Guess you might call it the universal way to start the day." Remi held out a mug of the steaming brew. She had opted for black, deciding he didn't look like a cream-and-sugar kind of guy. As he stepped closer to accept the coffee, she cautioned him. "It's hot."

"Heat does not bother me. When you live in a drafty castle on a windswept plain, you welcome heat." He raised the cup to his lips. "Even court it," he said over the rim.

For the first time, she noted the depth and richness of his voice. And that it was also smooth and sexy, like inky silk on bare skin.

With her gaze on his mouth, she licked her own lips. "Oh."

The corner of Dominic's mouth lifted in the faintest of smiles a second before he took his first sip. No matter the century, it seemed some things never changed. Men and women still wanted the same things. Namely, each other.

"I like this coffee of yours."

"Good. Are you, uh, hungry?"

Now it was his turn to gaze at her mouth. Her lips were full, and he wondered if they would be as soft as they looked. Would they yield to his quickly, or reluctantly? Would she yield immediately, or revel in love play? Unlike many of his fellow knights who considered women merely useful, he disliked too quick a conquest, preferring a long, sweet seduction. Remi's lips, like the rest of her body, would need lengthy and ardent attention, he decided.

"Aye," he said finally. "I am ravenous."

"Okay. Okay, that's good." Grateful to have something to occupy her hands, which had started to tremble, Remi turned and busied herself with preparing breakfast.

"May I have another draft of coffee?" Dominic requested as she set a plate of waffles and bacon in front of him.

"Sure." She refilled both of their cups. "Gotcha hooked, huh? Like I said, it's universal. In fact, if memory serves, England was inundated with coffeehouses in the seventeenth and eighteenth centuries. Very popular gathering places." She joined him at the table with her usual fare of a bran muffin and yogurt, plus an extra muffin for Dominic.

"You are very learned."

"Me? Hardly. I mean, my I.Q. is probably average. I just read a lot, and I've lived all over the world."

"All over the world?"

"Pretty much. Let's see..." Remi spread butter over her muffin, and thought for a moment. "We lived in the Valley of the Kings—that's in Egypt—with a tribe of aborigines in the Australian outback, Greece,

Crete, and then Paris, which was probably the closest thing to normal. Then there was Utah, Mexico, Africa. Oh, yeah, we even lived in England—London, to be specific—for two months while my father was lecturing there."

"And you were educated in all of these places?"

"Self-taught. When you move around as much as we did, you learn to teach yourself. My books were my best friends."

"And the rest of your family? You have no brothers or sisters?"

"An older brother. He's as eccentric as my folks."

"Ex—"

"You know, a few degrees off center, marches to the beat of his own drum . . ." At his exasperated expression, she stopped. "Sorry. I was going to try to hold it down, wasn't I? An eccentric," she said as if quoting from a dictionary, "is a nonconformist. Someone who is different from the norm. Odd."

"I see. And you are not one of these odd people?"

"I was, but I kicked the habit. My entire life has been spent in places most people have never heard of, much less been to. We rarely stayed in one location more than a year. Often only months. So, I made up my mind to find a home for myself and stay put. I've lived like a gypsy before. I don't recommend it."

"But you learned so much, saw so much."

"I learned how to be lonely. Learned how hard it was to make friends, harder still to leave them behind. Again and again."

Dominic, who had lived all but the first five years of his life at Kerwick Castle, couldn't imagine such a vagabond existence, particularly for a little girl. What ties did she have, save personal ones to members of her family? She called no place home. She had no history. Even though his lineage was not legitimate, it was long, and populated by honorable men. He found it hard to imagine her life as a child.

Except for the loneliness. They had that much in common.

He might have the roots she had longed for, but at least she could claim her father's name with pride.

"Children can be cruel, can they not?" he said softly.

"Yes." She glanced at him, and sensed that his comment was born out of firsthand knowledge. Had he been taunted as a little boy? And why?

"What about your family? Ohmygod," Remi said suddenly. "I never thought about it until now, but you could be married. With dozens of kids. Are you?"

Dominic grinned. "There is no wife." Then the grin faded. "And I assure you, there are no bastards."

The edge in his voice told her more than his words. "So, you left no one back in your time?"

"My mother."

Gripped by an overwhelming urge to know more about him, not just his history, but him personally, Remi forgot her breakfast. "Were you a happy little boy?"

The unexpected question startled him for a moment. "No one has ever asked me that question. Not then, or since."

"I'll bet you were the leader of all the other boys you played with. What about your father?" Remi knew her boldness bordered on bad manners, but her pressing need to know about him overrode etiquette.

"He was . . . he lived apart from my mother and I."

For a heartbeat, no more, she thought she glimpsed a longing in his eyes, a loneliness. Then he looked away.

"And you, my lady?" he asked, eager to draw her attention from him. "I see no husband. Has no man claimed you as his leman?"

"Leman? You mean, am I sleeping with someone? No, there is no man in my life."

"Good," he said before thinking. The news should not have thrilled him so, but it did. The thought of her in another man's arms was disquieting. He had envied men certain women before, but he had never experienced this feeling of possessiveness he felt where Remi was concerned. He wasn't sure he liked it.

"Good?"

"Aye. Any man worth his mettle would resent another man making demands on his woman's time, such as I am doing. If I were your lover, I would not allow it." When his eyes met hers, they were no longer remote, but as warm as the blue water of the Caribbean. "If I were your lover, nothing but war could take me from your side."

His voice slid over her senses like hot fudge over French vanilla ice cream. So seductive and so tempting that for a second or two Remi completely lost her train of thought.

"Well, uh, so you, uh, you grew up around the castle. Kerwick, that is."

"Aye."

"That's probably how you knew your way around Swords and Shields."

"Swords and Shields?"

"Where we were last night. The castle. It was moved here brick by brick, restored and modernized."

"It is possible to move an entire castle that has been standing in the same place for over five hundred years?"

"Sure. Piece of cake."

He glanced down at the muffin. "Nay. I have no appetite for cake."

"No." Remi laughed. "I didn't mean...never mind."

"Have many such castles been removed as you described?"

"I never gave it much thought, but probably a few." Seeing him frown, she asked, "Does that bother you for some reason?"

"'Tis only the thought of riding through my country past empty land where once stood a castle or keep. It feels strange and quite disrespectful."

"I know they exercised great care when the stones were transported. And the whole thing took almost two years, so you gotta figure they were careful."

"Still, it is disquieting."

"We were very sure to preserve everything just as it was. Anyway, I, uh, called you forth in the middle of a performance," she informed him, relieved to have moved to a more comfortable topic.

"A play?"

"Kinda. We do the same show every night, Monday through Saturday, plus a matinee on Saturday."

"It is always the same?"

"Pretty much. The actors switch from week to week, which knight they play, but otherwise it's basically the same every night."

"And you always play the enchantress?"

"Not always. I'm only in the performance when the regular actress doesn't show up."

"And the magic words you speak, are they always the same?"

"Uh, no. This time, I improvised . . . uh, added something. You see, my brother sent me a book of Druid chants for my birthday, which was yesterday, and I decided to include one of the chants in the performance." She sighed, pushing her plate away. "I know the Druids were reported to have had mystical powers, but I never in a million years thought there was any truth to it. I could kick myself for being so careless. I just opened the book, and started reading, never dreaming . . . Dominic," she said suddenly, her eyes misting. "You have to believe me. I—I didn't know what would happen. I'm so sorry I got you into this. My carelessness may have cost you everything, and I'll never forgive myself if—"

He didn't want to think about how high that cost could be. "Do you think you would know the words if you heard them again?" he asked.

"Maybe, but I wasn't kidding when I said messing with this stuff could be dangerous. I really don't know what might happen. It's very risky."

"A risk I must take," he said gravely. "Do we begin now?"

"Wouldn't you like to read the funny papers first?"

"What?"

Remi glanced down. "Never mind." Nervously, she began pleating the paper napkin beside her plate. "Just my feeble attempt at humor. You're tense, and I'm terrified. I thought it might lighten things up a bit."

"What frightens you?"

"Everything about this situation scares the hell out of me."

"Why?"

Her head snapped up. "Why? You could get killed, that's why." His eagerness to possibly meet his death made her angry. Couldn't he see the danger? "There's no telling how this time-travel thing will end. If I blow it, you could wind up as a snack for a T-rex or living with the Jetsons."

"I know not of these other...things, but I have faced death before."

"Well, I haven't, and I'd just as soon put the experience off as long as possible, thank you very much.

Particularly since I would be the one doing the killing." She shoved her chair away from the table, rose and headed for the sink.

"Remi."

The soft command in his voice stopped her cold. "What?" she said without turning around.

"I believe you."

She turned to face him. "You do?"

"Aye. And I do not blame you."

"Thank you. I *am* sorry. And you have my solemn oath that I will move heaven and earth to make things right."

"I believe that." He rose and walked to her.

"Thanks," she whispered, partly because she was genuinely relieved, and partly because when he got this close, she found him so, so . . . *near*. There was something terribly primitive and immediate about him. "I, uh, meant it when I gave my solemn oath." She held up her little finger. "Pinkie swear."

"Pinkie—"

"Hold up the little finger of your right hand." When he complied, the light glinted off the silver ring he wore. "Oh, cool ring."

"Nay," With his thumb he tested the metal. "It is warm from my flesh."

"No, by 'cool' I meant it was a great ring. Really nice."

"Your compliment is most gracious. It was a gift from my mother."

Remi smiled. "Think she'd mind her gift being involved in a pinkie swear? It's like a sacred promise."

"Nay." He smiled back. "Not in the least."

She hooked her finger around his, and looked into his eyes. "The most sacred promise."

"I accept, Mistress Balfour, with deepest gratitude."

They stood for a few long seconds, their fingers and gazes locked until, finally, Remi took her hand away. "Clothes," she said. "You need clothes."

"If you say so."

"Oh, yeah," she said, taking several steps backward. "We definitely need to get you covered."

"You have a tailor?"

"Lord, no. I can't afford handmade stuff. Not many people can. You know those buildings we passed last night?"

"Aye."

"Well, a couple of them have everything we'll need. Tell you what, I'll run up to Target and pick up some jeans, T-shirts, underwear. Maybe a pair of loafers, and some socks. I won't be long." She headed for her bedroom, then stopped and turned around. "But what size?"

"Size?"

"Oh, hell's bells, guess I'll just have to measure you, and compare the measurements to the sizes. Wait right here. I've got a tape measure in my office."

In seconds, she had returned with a long, thin strip covered with markings. "Okay, hold your arms out away from your body."

He obeyed, and she stepped up, slipped the measure around his chest, and noted the number. Then she did the same with his upper arms, neck, waist and length from his waist to the floor. She even measured the length and width of his feet. She had them all, but one.

His inseam—the length from crotch to floor.

"Dominic, I need to..." Remi swallowed hard, and licked her lips. "Take one last measurement."

"Please proceed."

"Well, this one is a little different from the others."

"How so?"

"I need to know how long your... I have to place the tape measure under, right next to your, uh..." She grimaced, bit the bullet and blurted out, "I need to measure the *inside* of your leg."

"Very well."

Easy for you to say, she thought, going down on one knee in front of him. "Would you move the sheet back a little—that's enough. That's fine," she assured him before he exposed more than she should see. What she could see was plenty. And she could see it at close range.

Since there simply was no graceful way to do this, she went about her task as calmly and quickly as possible.

Gazing at the crown of her head, Dominic smiled. Touching him made her nervous. It was a good sign.

"All done!" Remi practically shot up off the floor like a Saturn rocket off a Cape Canaveral launchpad.

When she stepped back, he noticed that her cheeks were bright pink.

"Back in a minute." She turned, and raced up the stairs to her bedroom.

A short time later, she came back down wearing another pair of shorts and another T-shirt. This one had the words All Stressed Up and No One To Kill on the front. She walked over to a cabinet, flipped open the door and reached inside. Suddenly, music filled the room.

"Thought you might like to listen to something classical while I'm gone."

"It is...wonderful." Dominic smiled, enjoying the soothing melody. "We often have players come to the castle, but nothing so grand as this." He glanced around. "Where are the musicians?"

Remi laughed. "In here." She opened the cabinet to reveal a CD player and other sound equipment. "The musicians play in a big hall, and the, uh—" she struggled for a word he might understand "—the music is engraved on these circles. Then we can play it over and over. Anytime we want. The sound comes out over there." She pointed to two speakers.

"It is like—"

"Don't say magic," Remi warned.

Dominic grinned. "A wonderful memory that you can relive whenever you choose."

"Thank you, kind sir." She inclined her head in a regal nod.

"Your servant, my lady."

He bowed, and should have looked ridiculous doing so, considering he was wearing nothing but a rumpled sheet. But he didn't. Remi had never seen anyone look more courtly or handsome in her life.

"Okay, enjoy the music. I'll be back as quick as I can. Oh, and if anything rings, buzzes or gongs, ignore it."

When she returned forty minutes later, he glanced up from the pages of a historical romance novel. On the cover was a dashing knight embracing a beautiful woman.

"Something made a noise," he said, pointing to her office.

Barely noticing he had dressed, Remi dropped her packages and headed straight for the fax machine. If they were lucky, it would be the response from one of the two information brokers she had contacted.

Well, Remi decided, there was luck. And then there was luck.

"What are you reading?"

Remi looked at Dominic standing in the doorway, filling the doorway actually, as he leaned against the framework. He was so vibrant, so alive. But for how long?

In her hand was a copy of a page from an obscure English history textbook printed in the 1920s. The last paragraph drew her attention as sharply as it had a moment ago. She read again, then a third time. She didn't have the heart to read on.

"Remi?"

"It's information about the battle," she told him, hesitant to meet his gaze. Fearful he would see the hopelessness in her eyes.

Instantly, he pushed away from the door, and came to stand beside her. "Pray tell, what does it say?"

"It's like I told you. Richard was defeated. Henry Tudor became Henry the Seventh."

"But there is more."

"Yes."

"Tell me, please."

"Y-your men all perished," she said softly.

"And I was among them?"

As an answer, she read the last few lines at the bottom of the page. "'Separated from the main force at Redmore Plain, a small band of Tudor supporters engaged Yorkist troops near Kerwick Castle. Though gallant to a man, the Lancastrians were soundly defeated and killed.'"

Dominic thought of all the brave men he had fought with so many times, and the widows and children they left behind. He thought of his squire, Erik. It had been his first and last battle. He prayed the young man's death had been swift and honorable. After all, what else could any man hope for?

"I did not expect to be well remembered."

"Yeah, guess most of us hope for a little more than a footnote in some dusty history book. There's another half a page," she said. "But it looks like just battle stuff. Is there anything else you need to know?"

"I would like to read the remaining account."

She handed him the paper.

"'The leader of the defeated troops was a knight known as Sir Dominic William Longmont, vassal to the Duke of Kerwick,'" he read. "'Noteworthy here only because he survived the battle, and was later instrumental in saving the life of Henry the Seventh.'"

"Let me see that." Remi all but snatched it from his grasp. "You survived. You didn't die."

She threw her arms around his neck, nearly toppling them both onto her desk. "See, I told you." Tears glistened in her green eyes. "You lived."

"Aye. As does the king." He held on to her, enjoying the feel of her in his arms, if only for the moment. "Tell me, does your paper tell of Henry as a good and just ruler?"

Remi scanned the page. "'The conflict'—meaning the Wars of the Roses—'was brought to an end by the victory of the Lancastrian heir, Henry Tudor, over Richard the Third at Bosworth Field in 1485,'" she read. "'The new king, Henry the Seventh, united the two houses by marrying Elizabeth of York, daughter of Richard's predecessor, Edward the Fourth.

"'It was a time of healing and peace. During Henry the Seventh's reign, commerce increased and the whole of the British Empire prospered."'" Remi looked up from the page.

"A time of healing," Dominic whispered. "Thank God."

"You saved the life of a man who brought peace and prosperity to England."

He sighed. "It is enough to know there is an end to the wars. An end to the dying."

"You've done—will do—your country a great service. Your single act of bravery will have far-reaching consequences."

"But not unless I return. If Henry dies, there could be war again."

"War would be the least of it," Remi told him. "If you don't go back and Henry dies, the whole course of history might be changed. And not just England's, but the world's."

They stared at each other, both suddenly overwhelmed with the gravity of the situation.

"We have to get you back. And the book is our only hope."

"LET'S TAKE A BREAK," Remi said two hours later.

They had concentrated on going through the Druid book one page at a time. Not reading the chants out loud, but with the help of several research volumes from Remi's library, selecting random words on each page and finding the definitions. This scattergun process was tedious at best, nonproductive at worst. So far, they hadn't found anything that even remotely sounded as though it was the chant they needed.

"I'm starving," she announced, stretching as she rose from the couch. "How about you?"

"Aye." He didn't look up from his perusal of the research book.

"Listen, I don't want you to worry." At that, he did glance up. "Pinkie swear, remember." She wiggled her little finger at him. "A promise is a promise. I'm going to do everything I can to get you back."

"Aye, I believe you are as good as your word."

He followed her into the kitchen where she made an incredibly delicious meal. Something she called a "sandwich," made with turkey meat and odd but tasty items called pickles and potato chips.

"I like your twentieth-century food," he said, taking a bite out of his second sandwich. "Does everyone in your time eat so well?"

"Oh, yeah, we're talking a feast here. No," she assured him. "This is plain, everyday stuff. Lots, and I mean, lots of people eat much better than this on a regular basis. Just like in your time, there are poor folks, not so poor, rich, very rich, and the obscenely wealthy."

"And they all live in the same city, close together as I saw when we were in your car?"

"Nope, most of the rich folks live in a much nicer neighborhood."

"Nicer?" He found it hard to believe that there were homes more luxurious than her condo.

"And bigger. Of course, we don't have too many castles, but we could give some of those big old English manor houses a run for their money."

"If I lived in your time, I would not want to live in a castle."

"Why not? Sounds pretty cool to me."

"Aye." He polished off the last of his sandwich. "And drafty."

Remi laughed. "Guess every life-style has its drawbacks. Now, me, I could use a long weekend in a castle. Someone to cook my meals, a chambermaid, maybe a coach and four—"

The sound of another fax arriving cut her off and she went into her office. Leaning over the machine, she read as the paper rolled up. "Dominic." Without taking her eyes from the page, Remi motioned him over.

"According to this, the assassination attempt on Henry was only about eight or ten days after the battle. It says that you were presumed dead, but your body was never found. And you fortuitously reappeared at Kerwick Castle while the king was in residence, foiled the attempt and killed the assassin. August 29, 1485."

"This is the same as the other report."

"No, Dominic. You don't understand. This is very specific, and I think the account is showing us positively that you came forward, then returned."

"I am not certain I—"

"Don't you see? You disappeared. Everybody thought you were dead, but they never found your body. You were just *gone*. Almost like you vanished into thin air, if you get my drift. Then, a week later, you *reappeared* in time to save the king. Coincidence?" With a hand on her hip, she shook her head. "I don't think so. This is proof that you came forward in time, *and* that you went back. Even the very day you returned."

"Does this mean that I cannot go back to my own time until then?"

"I think so. Trying before then might mess up some kind of time continuum. In fact, we should be very careful."

"Why?"

"If you should have an accident, say, break your leg or something, you might not be able to get back or save the king. History would be changed. Or . . ."

"Or what?"

"You could do something that might change the future."

"Such as?"

"You could accidentally meet a future president of the United States and influence him to grow up to be the president of Swords and Shields instead."

"Now I know you jest."

"Yeah, but all the same, I think we need to stick to the information we have. Of course, we still don't know *how* you go back. But we will figure it out. Says so right here."

"Your confidence inspires me, my lady."

"Well, don't get too confident. If my theory is right, you've—we've got a week to kill. So, temporarily at least, you are going to have to live in the twentieth century. And since Robert's Rules of Order don't exactly cover this situation, I guess we'll have to play it by ear."

"My ear?"

"*By* ear, it means..." Remi sighed. "Oh, never mind, just—"

"Trust you."

"'Fraid so."

"Do I have a choice?"

"'Fraid not. The question is, what in Sam Hill am I going to do with you until you disappear in a puff of smoke? One thing is for sure. I can't let you run around loose. No telling what might happen. So, you're stuck with me."

When she lifted her hands in a gesture of helplessness, her T-shirt stretched across her breasts, revealing the outline of what he thought might be lace. The idea that she wore lace, possibly even silk, beneath the strange and decidedly unfeminine clothing set his mind on things far removed from battles and kings. Indeed, he began wondering what it would be like to see the mysterious lace for himself.

Since he had no control over when he would return, Dominic decided that at least he could exercise some control over how he would spend the time until he returned. And if Remi didn't have any ideas, he most certainly did.

"Think you can stand having me practically under your nose for the next eight days?" she asked.

Dominic smiled down into her green eyes. "I think I will find such circumstances . . . bearable."

# 6

DOMINIC SOON discovered that living in Remi's time was easier than he had ever dreamed, beginning with what she called modern conveniences. The first one, the bathroom, he had already experienced that morning. The second was a shower.

"Have you ever taken a rainbath?" she asked, standing in front of the glass door to the shower. "You know, just stripped down and let the rain wash your body?"

"Aye, many times."

"This is the same deal, only you can turn the rain on and off."

"Truly? You can control the rain?"

"No, not the rain, but this is like . . . never mind, I'll show you."

With a twist of her wrist, water spurted from the shower-head. She tested the temperature. "Okay, once you've taken off your clothes, step in and shut the door. There's a bar of soap in the holder and a bottle of shampoo—" she pointed to her head "— on the hanging shelf. I'll leave a towel on the rack. When you're done, turn the knob to your right until the water stops. Got it?"

"Got it," he repeated.

"Whoa, better watch it or you'll be talking like me before long."

He grinned. "Have pity, mistress. You speak of a fate worse than death."

"Yeah, right. After you shower, we'll take a look at your new wardrobe."

Remi closed the door to the bathroom and started to walk away, but stopped. She stood listening, telling herself that she just wanted to make sure he didn't need any help. But that excuse didn't hold water and she knew it.

This was an invasion of privacy, she told herself. And rude. All true. All of which she ignored.

She heard the shower door snap shut. Then the volume of the water shifted from full to intermittent as he moved beneath the spray. She could imagine the stream of warm water sluicing over his hard body like a summer rain over chiseled rock. In her mind's eye, she could see his wet skin glistening as he lathered his powerful physique. And she could visualize his head thrown back under the spray, the water coursing down the strong column of his neck, across his chest, over his belly, down . . .

"Get a grip, Balfour. Next thing you know, you'll be drooling." She stalked into her office, flipped on her computer, went straight to the games menu and began a hand of solitaire, hoping to take her mind off her shameless fantasizing. It didn't work. She tried to put the ten of diamonds on the jack of hearts. After six more losing hands, she gave up and shut down the computer.

At almost the same time that she heard the shower being turned off, Remi remembered she hadn't mentioned to him about shaving. She jumped up, dashed down the hall . . .

And ran smack-dab into a cleaner, but once again half-naked, Dominic. The collision startled them, nearly unbalancing them both.

"Sorry—" She grabbed his upper arms.

"Your pardon—" He grabbed her shoulders. And held on.

"I, uh, wasn't watching where I was going," she said, her cheek inches away from his bare and still-damp chest, her heart thumping wildly against her rib cage.

"Nor was I." Her warm breath whispered across his skin, and he fought an overwhelming yearning for her to press her lips to his flesh, her body to his.

They stood so for several seconds, and when she didn't move away, he said, "Did you wish to speak with me?"

"What?" Remi looked up at him.

"Did you—"

"Oh, yeah. Shave. I thought . . . maybe you might shave. You know, your . . . face." She knew she sounded as though she didn't have two brain cells to rub together, but at the moment she couldn't seem to form a complete sentence.

"You are most gracious. I am humbled by your hospitality," he said, releasing her.

"Yeah, the, uh, razor and shaving cream are on the counter." She pointed to the bathroom then turned to go.

"Remi?"

She stopped. "Huh?"

"Since I am unaccustomed to your implements, could I prevail upon you to show me?"

"Oh, sure," she told him, realizing he had never seen an aerosol can before, much less a disposable razor. In some ways, having him around was like having a child to teach. But one glance at his body was all the reminder she needed that Dominic Longmont was a healthy adult male.

"As the cream comes out, it turns to foam," she demonstrated after he followed her back into the bathroom.

"Remarkable. And then what?"

"It goes on your beard, like this." Without thinking, she reached up and began spreading the foam over his face. In the process, her fingers accidentally skimmed over his mouth. Remi's hand froze.

Dominic's breath hit the back of his throat and he was instantly hard. Finding a level of control he didn't know he possessed, he carefully wrapped his fingers around her wrist and moved her hand away.

"You have a gentle touch."

"Th-thanks. I . . . you can probably take it from here." She slipped from his grasp and quickly rinsed off her hand. "Just don't cut yourself."

"I will take great care," he said as she disappeared out the door.

By the time he strolled into the living room thirty minutes later, Remi had her imagination and her heart rate under control. She wasn't accustomed to being in such close quarters with a man. Any man. It was only natural to be a little nervous. Add the fact that the man in question was a drop-dead gorgeous time traveler, and nervous barely covered it. She could handle the situation, she assured herself. No sweat.

"What is next in my transformation?" Dominic asked.

She had learned a valuable lesson with the inseam incident. This time, she found a way to get her point across without touching him, which was fast proving to be dangerous.

Remi handed him a stack of clothes consisting of a folded pair of prewashed jeans, a stone-washed hunter-green T-shirt and a package containing three pairs of underwear. On top of the stack she placed two pages ripped from a J. C. Penny catalog. One showed a man in jeans and T-shirt. The second showed a gorgeous hunk modeling men's underwear.

"Back to the bathroom. Study the pictures. This time, pal, you're on your own."

DOMINIC WAS AMAZED at how easily he adjusted to his new clothes, new surroundings. By the time they sat down to eat the evening meal—an odd, but wonderfully delicious food Remi called pizza—he was beginning to feel at ease in her time.

He liked twentieth-century garments. They fit his body like his leathers, yet they did not bind. Nor were they so heavy. The freedom was exhilarating, as heady as wine. Comfortable and sturdy, the fabric Remi identified as denim was nothing short of a miracle cloth, as far as Dominic was concerned.

But the word *miraculous* could be applied to everything in this new time. Everything he touched, tasted, heard and saw was exciting, fascinating. All of the items Remi called technology—the telephone, television, computer and many more—were astonishing. To think that these tools enabled her, or anyone, to speak to people not only in her own village, but in villages across her land, was, in Dominic's mind, truly magical. Because through them knowledge was spread far and wide, giving hundreds, maybe even thousands, an opportunity to have what only a pampered few had in his time.

"What did you do back in 1485 besides fighting the Yorkists?" she asked, polishing off the last slice of pizza.

"Do?"

"Yeah. Besides being a knight, I mean. Did you have a job or hold an office?"

"Nay."

"Well, we've got to find you something to keep you busy and out of trouble. Is there anything that you like to do or you're good at?"

"I am told I have a talent with falcons."

"We've got someone who works with the birds at Swords and Shields and he already has an assistant. You know horses, don't you?"

"To ride, train or groom?"

"Um, groom, probably. I know it's not much, but it will keep you occupied. And close to Navarr. Tim, the head groom, is easy to work for. Nobody will bother you. If that sounds okay to you, you're hired."

"Hired?"

Remi downed the last of her cola. "We hire people, pay them a wage."

"Money?"

"You better believe it. Everybody works. It's the great credo of the twentieth century. And how we put such a sumptuous feast—" she pointed to what was left of her own pizza "—on our table every night and pay the rent on our palatial mansions every month. There are no more serfs to grow food for the nobility." Well, that wasn't exactly true, but she didn't feel like giving him a lesson in tenant farming. "People go to work, get their money, then buy goods. Very much the same way tradesmen and merchants did in your time. Really, when you think about it, things haven't changed so drastically. The big difference is that the nobility is gone."

"And what became of them?"

"They're still hanging on in England, but we had a revolution and banned titles and nobility."

His eyes widened. "Truly?"

She made an X across her chest. "Cross my heart and hope to die. It's actually in our Constitution that nobody in this country can be titled. They did that so everyone would be equal."

"A most astonishing concept."

"It's worked pretty darn well for over two hundred years." She rose from the table, collected their empty plates and took them to the sink. "And speaking of work, that's what you'll have to do tomorrow. I'll take you in and introduce you to our wrangler and he can put you to work. How does that sound?"

"Acceptable."

"Gee, don't hurt yourself," she said, disappointed that he wasn't more excited at what she thought was a terrific solution to the problem of what to do with him.

"You think me ungrateful."

"You could say that."

During their meal, she had told him about the principles her country had been founded upon. A document called the Declaration of Independence which included a Bill of Rights for every man, woman and child born in her country. She had explained how her forefathers had fought for their right to live and worship as they pleased, and without persecution. How, in the years since, even though the system had not always been perfect, every citizen was granted these rights, regardless of race or heritage. According to Remi, a man was limited only by his imagination and determination.

The idea that a man born with nothing could, by his own initiative and not by his birth, become whatever he wanted touched a spark deep in Dominic's soul. And fear in his heart. The concept was both awesome and fearsome. No sworn allegiances, no dependency on king or lord. A man was his own king, his own master. Such freedom carried overwhelming responsibility.

Still, despite all she had told him, he wondered how much these rights translated to the real world. It was one thing to pass a law freeing slaves, but does that law free the *thought* of slavery in men's minds? Had the attitudes and morals of society evolved alongside the technology? Would his name still be blighted because he was a bastard? Regardless of her ideals, would Remi look at him any differently if she knew?

"The world you described—the one you live in every day—sounds like what I have always imagined heaven to be. Forgive me if I do not embrace something so wonderful without reservation. My whole life has been spent erring on the side of caution."

He was afraid. The realization startled Remi. The most fearsome-looking man she had ever seen, a powerful knight probably with scores of battles to his credit, was scared to face the unknown.

And why not? He was lost and out of place, with no frame of reference. If the situation were reversed, she had to admit that she would be knee-knocking, hand-wringing terrified.

"Well," she said, regretting she had been so quick to misjudge him, "I suppose a little caution is a healthy thing."

"I have found it to be so, my lady."

"Yeah, well. I'll take you to personnel first thing, then notify Clint."

"Clint?"

"Swords and Shields' head knight. He's responsible for everything that goes on in the arena. The actors, trainers, grooms all report to him. So that makes him your supervisor."

Dominic didn't think he liked the sound of anyone supervising him, but if it meant he could remain close to Remi, he could, as she would say, "deal with it."

REMI AND DOMINIC walked across the arena to where a tall blond man was talking to one of the eight knight/actors going through their daily rehearsal. "Good morning, Clint."

The blond man walked straight up to Remi and slipped his arm around her waist. "Good morning, sweet cheeks. How'ya doing?"

At the endearment, a sudden violent rage boiled through Dominic, followed closely by an overwhelming urge to thrash the man within an inch of his life. The feelings were so strong, so powerful, and so unexpected, it took him a second to recognize them.

Jealousy.

He was jealous of this man touching Remi.

Remi stepped smoothly out of Clint's hold, glancing up at Dominic. His gaze, hard as stone, bored into the other man.

"Dominic, this is Clint Hogan, our head knight."

"Clint, this is Dominic Longmont. He's going to be working with Tim in the stables."

The incredulous expression on Clint's face didn't surprise Remi. The last time he saw Dominic, he was out cold after disrupting the show and being carried away by the knights.

Clint looked Dominic up and down. "You sure this is a good idea, Remi?"

"Yes."

Remi noticed Dominic's rigid posture and the way the muscles in his neck stood out, as though they were embossed on his skin.

Oh, no, she decided, seeing the tension between the two men. This wouldn't do. She had better explain the situation to Clint right now.

"Clint, could I have a word with you?" she said, taking aside the head knight.

Dominic watched her for a moment, knowing she was doing her best to convince Hogan to accept the cover story she had insisted would work. Namely, that his unexpected appearance at last Saturday evening's performance had been a desperate attempt to get a job.

He loathed the idea of her pleading with anyone on his behalf, but at the moment, he wasn't certain his loathing stemmed from wounded pride or the fact that he didn't want Hogan, or any man, standing so close to Remi. She had told him there was no man in her life, yet this man acted very familiarly toward her.

He had to bring his emotions under control, not to mention his lust, he told himself. Where she was concerned, he was treading on dangerous ground. Nothing could come of his feelings for her. She belonged to the present, and he to the past.

He glanced to the far end of the arena where a falcon was tethered to a perch. Even hooded, the bird appeared nervous, agitated. Dominic looked back at Remi who was still talking to a frowning Clint Hogan, then headed for the falcon.

"You know, I'm as sympathetic as the next guy, but couldn't we just give him the number of the Texas Employment Commission and send him on his way?" Clint said at the end of Remi's explanation.

"I'm not sure that's wise," she told him. "What if he decided to sue us? The guy wants to be a knight because he thinks it's glamorous. He probably thinks the women will be lining up to date him."

"Well, he's in for a surprise. This is hard work. He's screwy if he thinks he can come in here and become a star overnight."

"Exactly," she said firmly. "What if he is unbalanced? Just think of all the bad publicity he could generate with a lawsuit. The public is biased when it comes to corporations. If this guy turns into a media clown, we could be in major trouble."

"So the big bosses have decided to pamper him, huh?"

"His horse, too."

"You've got to be kidding."

"They're a package deal," she said. "But not to worry. I don't think he'll hang around long. Working in the stables is not nearly as glamorous as being in the arena. I give him a week at the most."

"All right, but I wanna go on record. I don't like it."

"So noted. And thanks, Clint."

One hurdle down and no telling how many more to go, Remi thought, spotting Dominic at the other end of the arena. As she approached him, she heard him talking softly to the falcon.

"You are beautiful. Magnificent," he said, pulling on the leather gauntlet he had retrieved from one end of the perch. "Your wings are swift, your eyes keen. You are mistress of the air." He stroked his fingertips over the peregrine's head, wings and breast, his touch gentle and certain. Tiny bells tinkled as the falcon moved on her perch, cocking her head at the sound of the soothing voice.

"You have more than a talent," Remi said, keeping her voice low so as not to alarm the bird. "You have a gift. Maybe I should ask Clint to let you work with the birds."

"I fear your friend might not agree," he said, continuing to stroke the falcon.

"Don't worry about Clint. He went along with our story. And what was that killer stare for, anyway?"

"Stare?"

"At Clint. For a minute there, I thought you were going to punch his lights out."

"What lights?"

"You know, smack him." She clipped him ever so lightly on the chin. "Knock his block off."

Dominic captured her delicate fist and held it. "Should I have? Is he a former lover?"

The question almost shocked Remi speechless. "L-lover!"

"Aye. It is a plain enough question."

Until that moment, he hadn't realized how important her answer was. He held his breath, anticipating the worst, praying for the best.

"Have you lost your—"

"He touched you with familiarity."

"Familiarity?"

"Aye. Are all men in your time accustomed to touching a beautiful woman in this manner, or is it merely Hogan that is so bold?"

"Oh, you mean when he put his arm..." His words finally sank in. "Y-you think I'm beautiful?"

"Aye. As a spring day," he said, his voice as soothing as when he had spoken to the peregrine. "And as graceful as flowers in a breeze. You have the face of an angel and the body of a temptress. It is easy to see why men would want to touch you."

He did. He wanted to touch her at that very moment. And he wanted to keep on touching her until they were both on fire with need.

She gazed up at him, her eyes wide, wondering. "No one has ever called me those things before."

"Have they not, my lady?" He removed the gauntlet and using the same hand he had used to gentle the bird, he brushed a curl from her cheek. "Then perhaps the men of your century would do well to take lessons from the men of mine."

REMI DIDN'T REMEMBER what she said after that. Or what Dominic said. Or if either of them said anything at all. The only thing she remembered was the tenderness in his touch and the passion in his eyes. A look so passionate her body tingled with warmth and . . . anticipation. And even though the feelings were not ones she experienced on a daily basis, she had no problem identifying them.

Attraction, allure, desire, animal magnetism— dress it up any way you wanted, but it still came down to plain old-fashioned lust. And two hours after the fact, she was still warm from the glow.

Remi stared at her monitor, watching the cursor flash. She hadn't been able to work since her conversation with Dominic.

"Conversation?" she mumbled. "More like he talked and I drooled."

The truth was, their brief, but oh so arousing "conversation" had changed things. At least for Remi. Before Dominic rode into her life, she had always been confident that keeping her heart and body untouched for all these years had been right for her.

She knew some of her women friends thought her strange, they didn't understand her self-imposed chastity. But then, how could they, unless they had lived the life she had? It had to do with spending her childhood tagging along in the wake of her parents' wanderlust. It had to do with never feeling as if she had any control over her life. It had to do with permanence and security. But more importantly, it was about happily ever after. And forever. So, maybe it was a fairy-tale dream. It was her dream.

That's why she was so confused.

Dominic was everything she ever dreamed about. Prince Charming, a knight in shining armor. And he wanted her. She could see it in his eyes, feel it in the way he touched her.

But he wasn't, and could never be, the fulfillment of her dream. He wasn't forever.

Yet, her heart was telling her he was the one.

She had always known love would happen like this, quick and breathless. As if someone had jerked a rug from beneath her feet. She had always known that when she fell, she would fall like the proverbial ton of bricks. Only, she had expected to fall in love with a man that would be around for a while.

What a cruel twist of fate, she thought. The only forever that applied to Dominic was that in a few short days he would be gone from her life. Forever.

Now all she had to do was keep her emotions in check until Dominic was gone. All she had to was pretend that she hadn't fallen hopelessly in love with him. She was a sometime actress, she could pull it off. Couldn't she?

Remi switched off her computer, rose from her desk and checked her watch. She had promised Dominic they would have lunch together. After checking on him several times this morning—all without his knowledge—she was satisfied that he would be well occupied and able to handle working with the other men. During the day she would have little problem keeping up the pretense. But what about the nights?

NAVARR CAUGHT his master's scent as he drew near, snorting and stamping his feet in acknowledgment. All the other grooms had gone home and the stable was quiet, almost peaceful.

"How are you, my brave friend? Still confused?" The stallion tossed his head and Dominic laughed. "Aye. That makes two of us. You are lucky. Your confusion is only time and place. Mine includes people."

He rubbed the velvety nose. "I should not have spoken so to Remi," he told the horse. "What madness was I contemplating?"

*Madness.*

An appropriate word, for surely, if a man could be driven mad with desire for a women, he was that man.

"She is a rare woman. So soft and so tempting. And forbidden."

At the dark tone of Dominic's voice, Navarr again tossed his head, his nostrils flared. "That is how I must think of her now. I must forbid myself from wanting her warm and willing beneath me."

He sighed. "But how does one forbid lust?"

Or longing. For that matter, how did one forbid the heart to yearn?

"I have never known such feelings for any woman. For anyone," he told the animal. "This deep longing to be with her, simply to hear her voice, is like a revelation. Profound and frightening all at once. I fear, my friend, that I have lost my heart."

The only thing Dominic could compare these new feelings to was his soul-deep need to be recognized by his father. That need had been the guiding force in his life. Until now.

Until Remi.

As much as he would like to have kept her to himself for the brief time they had left, a part of him was relieved not to be concerned about having to fight his urges for a few hours in the day. The nights, however, were of great concern.

# 7

"I'VE GOT SOMETHING special planned for you tonight. A treat."

Dominic's mind took a quick flight of sensual fantasy before he reined in his erotic thoughts. "And what, my lady, might that be?"

"You'll see. It's a surprise."

He smiled. "I cannot remember the last time I received a treat, even as a child."

"Can't fool me. All little boys love surprises. Big boys, too," she added as they pulled into her driveway.

She didn't mention her special plan all through their evening meal, and he began to wonder if she had forgotten. She did, however, smile continuously, as if she held a secret.

"Great chow," he said at the end of dinner.

"Where in the world did you learn that word?"

"One of the knights. When he returned from his midday repast—"

"Lunch, and they're not really knights."

"Aye. When he returned from lunch, he patted his belly and proclaimed the food he had eaten with a greasy spoon to be 'great chow.'"

Remi laughed. "You're priceless, you know that?" She carried their plates to the sink.

Dominic sidled up to her. "Enough to ransom my surprise?"

"Ah, and sneaky, too. Thought you could take 'em or leave 'em."

"Truth be told, I would rather take them," he admitted a little sheepishly. "Good thing this news will never reach my men."

"Oh, my lips are sealed." She smiled up at him, enjoying the lighthearted moment. Dominic was much too somber for his own good. She had told him on more than one occasion to lighten up, but clearly he didn't know how. It was time he had some fun.

"So," he prompted.

"So what?"

"You are going to force me to ask you, are you not?"

"Force? A little bitty thing like me, forcing a big ole man like you?"

"You do intend to torment me."

"Just a little."

"And for how long?"

"Oh—" she checked her watch "—about five more minutes. About the time it takes for you to change your clothes."

"Why must I change my clothes?"

She pointed to his jeans. "Because you can't go swimming in those. You do swim, don't you? It's okay if you don't," she hurried to assure him. "I can teach you."

"That will not be necessary."

Swimming, Dominic thought, looking at himself in the bathroom mirror a few minutes later. As a boy in the south of France, swimming had been one of his greatest pleasures. When he and his mother had moved to England, he had known that simple pleasure less and less because of the harsh climate. As a vassal to the duke, he had found little time for such frivolous pursuits.

On Remi's instructions, he had discarded his jeans for another pair that had been transformed into "cutoffs," courtesy of her scissors. As a child, he had always swum naked, but she assured him that would not be the case tonight.

When he came out of the bathroom, she was nowhere in sight, and he assumed she was still changing her clothes upstairs. "Are you certain this is the correct attire?" he called up the stairway.

"It's called a bathing suit, more or less," came her reply.

"But we are not bathing."

"I know, it's just—"

"An expression," he finished just as she came down the stairs.

"Right."

He eyed her T-shirt and bare legs.

"And before you ask, *my* bathing suit is underneath my shirt. C'mon. I promised you a treat."

She took his hand and led him out the back door of the condo, through the backyard gate and around the building to the Olympic-size pool. The usual day-time sun worshipers had long since left, and they had the pool to themselves.

"Well, whadaya think?" She tossed the towels onto a nearby chair, then grabbed the hem of her T-shirt and pulled it over her head.

"I think," Dominic said, his eyes sparkling with pleasure as he turned to her. "That . . ."

That she was beautiful.

So beautiful she stole the breath from his lungs, and speech from his lips. Dominic stared at her, stunned by her beauty. He had grown accustomed to her bare legs in a pair of shorts, but this was . . .

She was all but naked except for a small amount of white fabric stretched over her body like a second skin. But it took less than a heartbeat for his shock to turn to admiration, and admiration to something much more physical. Her body was flawless. Sleek, slender and flawless. She was a goddess in the flesh.

"Dominic?"

"Aye," he whispered.

"That's the deep end. This is shallow. You ready to hit the water?"

He nodded, praying the water was cold enough to chill the blood rushing to his loins.

IT WASN'T nearly cold enough to suit Dominic. And after watching Remi dive beneath the surface, then glide through the water like a silver leaf floating on moonlight, the temperature would have had to be below freezing to affect his aroused body. He dived into the deep end of the pool, remaining below the surface for as long as he could.

"Who taught you how to swim? Your father?" she asked when his head broke the surface.

"My grandfather. But we moved to England when I was five, and there was little opportunity to swim after that." Dominic swam to the opposite side of the pool.

He almost groaned out loud when she followed him. Did she not know what effect she was having on him? Could she not see? And if he had desired her before seeing her in a bathing suit, that desire had now become a pounding need.

"Hey!" She splashed him playfully. "Let's race," she shouted, trying to get a head start.

"Vixen," Dominic called, not sure how much speed he could generate in his condition.

They raced from one end of the pool to the other. Once. Twice. A third time. Dominic was grateful for the strenuous exercise. By the time he had won the third race, he was feeling much more relaxed, even playful.

Breathing deeply, she swam up next to him in the deep end. "You cheated." She splashed him.

He splashed her back. "And you, mistress, are a poor loser."

"Am not. I would have taken you if you didn't have the strength of ten men, not to mention those Mr. Universe muscles in your legs."

"A knight must have strength as well as honor."

"Well, you've got it. In spades." She flicked a spray of water in his face, then quickly shoved away from the edge of the pool and sank beneath the surface before he had a chance to retaliate.

But Dominic was too quick for her. He reached underwater, caught her and hauled her up against him so fast she came up sputtering. So fast that it was a moment or two before she realized that she was practically lying on top of him as they floated, her legs moving slowly between his, treading water.

One of his hands was on her shoulder, the other at her waist. She could feel the heat from his touch through her bathing suit, through her body. He was holding her close, yet being careful to keep her gently suspended in the water.

The instant Dominic felt her body against his, he knew that he had made a grave error. But an even greater error would be to pursue his desire. Yet, how did he convince his body not to respond to her full, lush breasts that begged to be touched? To her nicely rounded derriere that was meant to be stroked. To her long, sleek legs that belonged around him. How did he convince his body to ignore such temptations?

The power of the man holding her sank into Remi's senses, sang through her blood. She glanced at his hand on her shoulder, wide, strong, and a feeling of assurance swept over her. She was in the arms of a man from another time, floating in eight feet of water, and she had never felt more secure in her life.

"Your hands are so big and strong," she said, unintentionally voicing her thoughts.

Immediately, he moved his hand. "Have I hurt you?"

"No! Oh, no." She looked at his face now cast in shadows as the moon passed behind a cloud. "It's just that when you touch me I feel small and fragile. Protected. I'm not used to that feeling."

"You do not like feeling protected?"

"I'm not sure. When you've been on your own for as long as I have, it's hard to trust someone else to care for you."

"But the day will come when you will trust a man."

"I suppose so, as long as he doesn't take advantage of my vulnerability."

He lifted a wet strand of hair from her neck in a gesture reminiscent of the way he had touched her cheek that afternoon in the arena. His fingertip lightly stroked the rim of her ear. "If I were the man you chose, I would cut out my heart before I would hurt you."

Her arms encircled his neck and his hands drew her closer, sending lightning strokes of need through her body.

"Would you? That's a very chivalrous thing to say." Their lips were so close. "It is true."

In a matter of seconds, the world had become a very small place. All that existed was him, her, and need. The need to be touched, kissed.

"I sure hope so. Kiss me, Dominic," she murmured a second before her lips touched his.

His mouth covered hers, his tongue seeking hers in the most ancient and intimate of duels. A battle of heat and passion. And the struggle continued until she was breathless, and totally lost in the kiss. Lost to the give and take of white-hot need that fed upon itself.

Remi had never known the kind of pleasure Dominic offered, a pleasure that gathered deep inside her and burned like a flame, growing hotter with each stroke of his tongue. She wanted more. More pleasure, more heat.

Since the moment he had left his own time, Dominic had felt powerless to control his life. Now he was in control. This he knew. This was real. Yet, even as he felt power surge through his body, he felt no need to overpower, to dominate. Instead, he felt impelled to claim what had been preordained as his, as part of his soul, his heart, his very being.

He groaned, taking the kiss deeper as his hands explored the contours of Remi's body, skimming over the outer curves of her breasts, then her waist and hips. His hands spread wide across her bottom, and urged her closer still, allowing her to feel the strength of his desire while he continued to ravage her willing mouth. Using his lips, teeth and tongue, he applied his expertise with deliberate care, and gratifying results.

She met him nibble for nibble, thrust for thrust until neither knew where one ended and the other began.

Remi's senses were completely absorbed in the kiss. Time, distance, night or day. None of it had any meaning. The only thing that mattered was the feel of Dominic's mouth on hers, his hands on her body. So much so that only when she lifted her legs to wrap them around his waist, did she realize how far they had gone. How close she was to giving herself to him right then and there.

"Please," she begged, not sure if she was begging him to stop or to continue.

"You taste like honeyed wine. Sweet, intoxicating." He nipped at her lower lip, full and wet from his kisses.

They had floated to the shallow end of the pool, and Remi was finally able to stand on her own, physically, then mentally.

"We must stop," she said, breathless and trembling.

"I need you." He trailed kisses down her neck, and back to her lips.

"I know, and I . . ."

His head dipped, and she felt his tongue glide over the swell of her breasts just above the neckline of her swimsuit. The sound she made fell somewhere between a gasp and a sigh.

"Dominic . . . Dominic . . ."

The sound of her voice breaking as she called his name finally penetrated the sensual haze clouding his brain, and brought reality into sharp focus.

"Remi." He pulled her into a fierce embrace. "Forgive me. I have shocked you, forced you—"

"No." She drew back, touching her finger to his warm lips. "I wanted you to kiss me. I asked you to kiss me even though I knew it was wrong. This is insane. We can't do this."

"You are right," he said, struggling to bring his lust under control. "We cannot do this." He held her face in his hands and looked deeply into her eyes. "Can we?"

"N-no."

The wealth of sadness and regret in that one word cooled Dominic's ardor like nothing else could. If he pressed her, she would yield. He knew it as well as she did. But at what price? What could he offer her but more sadness? Her life was here and now. His was long ago. He had nothing to give her except temporary pleasure and he would not allow his lust to overshadow his honor. Honor was all he had, and meant more than life itself. He must not do this.

With a sigh, he touched his forehead to hers. "The time and circumstances are wrong. You should have a man who can give you the roots and stability of heritage that you deserve."

Slowly, carefully, he released her, and together they climbed the steps out of the water. Without another word, they dried off then left the pool area, and returned to the condo.

"I'll take that." She reached for his damp towel as they stepped into the kitchen. "Why don't you get dressed, and after I change we'll go back to work on the chants. We don't have much time."

"Aye," was all he said, knowing that time, the very thing that had brought them together, was now their enemy.

While she dressed, Remi promised herself she would avoid any more close encounters of the personal kind. They had a mutual purpose. To return him to the right time so that he could save a king. And it was a noble purpose. Certainly finer than . . .

Than what? she thought, stepping into her shorts. Making love? Her head told her she was right, but her heart kept wondering if anything could be finer than loving Dominic.

"THIS ONE LOOKS promising," Remi said some time later as she pored over the chants.

"You think it is the one?" Dominic asked from the chair across from her. Quickly, he abandoned his mechanically reproduced copy of pages of the book—another of her twentieth-century miracles—and joined her on the sofa.

"I'm not sure, but the words I've picked all indicate a call to someone. Maybe we hit pay dirt."

"Show me."

"Here." She thumbed through the ancient Celtic dictionary opened on the coffee table before her until she found the right page. "This word—" she pointed to one in the Druid book "—means bold or fierce. And I think this one means champion or hero. That's a major part of the dialogue for that part of the show, me calling the knight to battle." She glanced up, her eyes sparkling with enthusiasm. "Lookin' good, huh?"

"I believe so."

"And I'm betting this one—" she flipped to the next page and pointed to a word "—means come, or call forth. Keep your fingers crossed."

Hurriedly searching through the dictionary, Remi could barely contain her excitement. This was it, she just knew it. "Here it is!"

Then her smile drooped. "That doesn't sound right. Oh, no." Disappointed, she slumped back on the sofa. "Wrong chant."

"Are you certain? Perhaps you should look again."

"Oh, the words mean fierce, and champion, all right, but not in the way we need them to. It's a love chant."

"A what?"

"Love chant. Obviously, the words have more than one meaning, like in the Greek language." She began to straighten the papers and notes scattered around the research books. "It, uh, is to call forth a fierce champion of . . . love. Uh, a bold lover."

There followed a long silence before Dominic said simply, "Perhaps it is the right one, after all."

Remi's head snapped up. "I don't . . . I don't think so."

His hand on hers stilled her nervous activity. "Are you so sure?"

Was she? Had she conjured up the warrior lover of her fantasies? Had she longed for her very own knight in shining armor so much that her yearning, combined with the chant, had brought him to her?

"Remi?" She was so close. He fought the urge to haul her into his arms, to taste her lips again, knowing he must resist it.

Even now, she longed for him to kiss her again, knowing it would only lead to pain. The mere touch of his hand on hers recalled the way he had stroked her body as she floated in his embrace. He was so close. If she leaned forward a few inches . . .

"Yes," she whispered, fighting the overwhelming urge to move closer. "I—I suppose it's possible this could be the one." Slowly, reluctantly, she slipped her hand from beneath his. "But I think we should keep looking just to be on the safe side."

"Of course."

His voice sounded so cold and remote she wanted to cry. Then he moved back to the chair, and she felt almost abandoned. Which was ridiculous, she told herself. He was only a few feet away. But she wanted him beside her again. She wanted him next to her, holding her . . . Suddenly, she couldn't sit there another minute without bursting into tears or begging him to take her in his arms again. She had to get out of the room.

"I think we've done enough for tonight. We'll try it again as soon as we get home from work tomorrow. Good night, Dominic." And she hurried from the room.

Dominic watched her leave and desperately wanted to call her back. He wanted to go after her. He wanted . . .

What he couldn't have. Not as long as he belonged in another time.

He yanked out the futon and made his bed so furiously the sheets were barely secure when he finished. He didn't care. After stripping to his underwear, he jerked back the sheets, got into bed and stared at the ceiling.

*Not as long as I belong in another time.*

What was truly strange was that he didn't feel, had never felt, as if he belonged in his own time. For as long as he could remember, he had felt like an outsider in the land of his father. He accepted the customs, and had been accepted by his peers, yet he had never experienced a oneness with the land and the people.

The only person he was close to was his mother, and she understood his feelings because she shared them. Since the day his father, the duke, had sent for him and his mother, they had lived comfortably. Luxuries were few, but Alise Longmont taught her son that the needs of the soul often outweighed the needs of the body. Dominic had everything he needed. Except, of course, the one thing he wanted above all else. His father's recognition.

Strangely enough, staring up at the darkened ceiling of Remi's living room, even that seemed less important now. Indeed, it seemed as if it belonged in some other man's life, not his. This time, this place . . . all of it seemed to be more real to him than his life in the past.

It was exciting, exhilarating. And not only because of all the marvelous inventions, but because of the personal freedom.

Here a man could claim his honor without having to defend it. A man could be whatever he chose to be. A choice dependent more on his determination than his lineage. Unquestionably, prejudice had survived, even thrived into this century, human nature being what it was, but still freedom was all around. In this time, this world, there was no limit to what a man could become.

*And with a woman such as Remi beside me . . .*

Suddenly, Dominic realized how far he had allowed his daydream to progress. Until that moment, he had not realized how much he longed for such a reality.

If only he could remain with Remi. If only . . .

*Come to your senses, man! Such dreams are not possible.*

He had a responsibility he could not set aside, and these longings were the worst kind of self-inflicted torture. It took little imagination for him to envision a life with Remi, a life of freedom to be his own man. A man she could love and respect. A man she could truly love.

"Aye," he whispered. "There lies your dream. There lies your truth."

His last thoughts before falling asleep, impossible as he knew them to be, were of the future. A future that belonged to him and Remi, together.

CLINT HOGAN STROLLED past the mews at the end of the stables, and stopped at the corner, where Dominic was working with a falcon.

"You were hired to work with the horses, not the falcons, Longmont."

In the process of getting the peregrine to come to his wrist, Dominic kept his voice soft and even, despite the fact that he would like nothing better than to tell Hogan to be gone. Permanently.

"I suggest you stick to—"

"Clint," Remi called as she entered the stable area. "They need you in the office."

"Comin', sweet cheeks." He glared at Dominic. "Mind what I'm telling you, Longmont, or—" he jerked his head in Remi's direction "—assistant manager or no assistant manager, you're gonna wind up out on your keester."

It took all of Dominic's willpower not to respond. Not to tell the so-called head knight what he thought of him, which was precious little. Instead, he returned Hogan's glare.

Clint turned and walked back to where Remi was standing.

Dominic was about to resume his work with the peregrine, when he noticed that Clint had put his arm around Remi as he had the day before. Unlike the previous time this had occurred, she didn't move away. A second later, Hogan leaned forward as if to whisper something in her ear.

Then, to Dominic's utter shock, they laughed. He could hear the soft, musical sounds of Remi's laughter even from his end of the stable. His hands balled into fists, and rage flashed through his body. Surely a man such as Clint Hogan could hold no interest for her. She deserved someone better.

Better than himself? Better than a man who could offer no future?

What right did he have to make such judgments? In a few days he would be gone, never to be a part of her life again. He would be in his own time, and she would be left here. What right did he have to say who belonged in her life, and who didn't?

None.

Yet the thought of another man touching her, making love to her, nearly drove him to the edge of insanity. It was then he knew that he had fallen deeply in love with her. The very thing he had fought to avoid, he must now face squarely. He was hopelessly in love with Remi.

AT LUNCHTIME Remi went in search of Dominic and found him already sharing hamburgers and french fries with some of the knights in the employees' lounge. For a moment, she considered joining them, which wasn't unusual, but she decided against it.

From the smile on his face, he was obviously enjoying being with the other men. After all, he was accustomed to a certain amount of camaraderie, and perhaps he missed it. No, Remi thought, let him enjoy himself. Still, she was disappointed.

When she was required to stay late that night to work on the books, she offered to drive Dominic home.

"Why must you stay?"

"Clint and I have to go over the quarterly budget figures. They have to be turned in to our manager by next week."

"Only you and Hogan?"

"Yes."

"I will wait."

Remi shrugged. "Suit yourself. I just thought you could have a couple of hours to work on the chants before I got home."

"Nay."

"Well, excuse me," Remi said at his flat refusal. "I wasn't trying to palm off all the work on you." And she stalked off.

He had been in a strange mood all day, and she had finally decided it had to be the kiss. He probably wasn't used to women asking to be kissed then wrapping their legs around his waist. The women of his time were gentle, nonaggressive creatures who did as their fathers or husbands told them to do. The history books didn't refer to them as chattel for nothing. Maybe he felt she was too assertive, that she had somehow tried to unman him. The idea sounded a little crazy for a modern woman, but it made sense for a medieval man.

While she was waiting for Clint, Remi took some carpet samples she was considering for the lounge area of the newly repainted ladies' rest room to her car. The samples were bulky, so she decided to put them in her trunk. When she opened it, there was Dominic's forgotten armor, shield and sword, from his first night.

Gazing at it, she couldn't help remembering the way he had looked as he bolted through the smoke screen, so dashing. Even then she had known he was different. She had instantly recognized that he was not the assigned actor. That moment seemed like weeks past, she thought, shoving aside his armor to make room for the samples. As she did, his shield came into full view.

A shield with a bar sinister across the crest.

Remi stared at the wide band of color, knowing it meant the wearer was a bastard. Illegitimate.

Bar sinister. Two words providing a clear picture of his circumstances. No doubt a young maid had caught the eye of the lord of the manor, and Dominic was the result. The story was as old as Adam and Eve. He wasn't the first illegitimate child, and history certainly supported the fact that he wasn't the last.

Suddenly, her heart broke. No wonder Dominic thought the twentieth century was such a marvelous place. In his time, a bastard was usually an outcast. And openly displayed for contempt, as evidenced by the bar sinister.

*You should have a man who can give you the roots and stability of heritage that you deserve.*

Dominic's words rang in her head as she closed the trunk and went back inside.

SHE AND CLINT WORKED through the performance, and for a half hour afterward until they finished. It was almost eleven o'clock, and as quickly as she could, she went looking for Dominic, but he was nowhere to be found. Where could he have gone? And at that hour? He couldn't drive, and he had never been anywhere without her. Frantic, she was on the verge of rounding up several of the remaining employees to help her look, when one of the departing actors informed her that Dominic had gone with some of the guys to Slim's, a bar several blocks away.

Remi was furious.

"How dare he go off to some bar when his life and the life of the king of England are hanging in the balance?" she muttered, whipping her Mustang out of the parking lot, headed for Slim's. "That's just like a man. He's got ten minutes to kill, and he heads for the nearest watering hole."

Remi knew she was being unreasonable, judgmental and at least a dozen other things, but she didn't care. Dammit, he had no business going off without telling her. He should've . . .

What? Checked in with her? Invited her along?

*All of the above?*

Remi couldn't decide which hurt more, him not telling her where he was going, or going without her.

*Get real. You just wanted him to want you to go along.*

She squirmed under the pressure of the truth. Since the moment he had ridden through the smoke and into her life, they had been together. She felt connected to him in a way she'd never felt connected to another human being, including her family. Particularly her family. It didn't matter that in a few days they wouldn't be together at all. Ever. It hurt to think that he wanted to be without her now.

Of course, that didn't mean she wasn't still mad. She was. Mad as hell, in fact.

She was so upset, so distracted, she neglected to notice that she'd parked beneath a nonfunctioning light standard. In fact, Slim's parking lot had several lights out, some areas too dark to see someone approaching until they stepped into the light.

She spotted the men the moment she walked into Slim's, and headed straight for their table. Play it cool, she told herself. She didn't want to embarrass or humiliate Dominic in front of the other guys, but she was determined to talk to him. Something was wrong. And she intended to find out what it was.

"Hey, Remi." One of the guys got up and offered her his chair. "C'mon join us. How about a beer?"

"No, thanks, I, uh, personnel had some papers they needed Dominic to fill out and they, uh, didn't have his home number." It was a lame excuse, but it was the best she could come up with on such short notice. She glanced at Dominic, practically daring him to object.

So, Dominic thought, she was an accomplished liar as well as a flirt. He had not been able to get the image of her laughing with Clint Hogan out of his mind. When one of the actors had suggested going to what sounded like a tavern, and "tossing down" what sounded like strong drink, he had gratefully accepted. The contents of at least four of the highly recommended "long necks" had passed his lips and he was pleasantly relaxed.

"Uh-oh, Nick," one of the other actors teased. "The boss lady has hunted you down. You musta been a bad boy."

"Or a very good boy," another added.

Remi threw the actor a lethal look. "Could I talk to you outside, Dominic?" She turned and walked away, fully expecting him to follow. He did, but he took his own sweet time.

"Just what the hell do you think you're doing?" she hissed as soon as he joined her just outside the door.

"Sharing a moment of relaxation."

"How many beers have you had?" Here she was, worrying about him and he was out having a good time. Her barely leashed fury broke free.

"That, mistress, is none of your business."

"We're going home," she insisted, prepared to drag him across the poorly lit parking lot.

"I have been invited to dine with my new friends."

"Now, listen, Dominic—"

"Some place with the name of an owl. No, not the name, the sound. Hoot—"

Remi's mouth dropped in shock. "Hooters! You're going to Hooters!"

The eatery was famous not so much for its food as its waitresses. All of whom wore tight short shorts, and even tighter T-shirts tied up under their well-endowed chests. The place was always packed, and the clientele was, predictably, at least ninety percent male. Anyone who came to Hooters for the food was new in town.

"Aye, I believe that is the place."

"Over my dead body. That does it. You're coming with me." Remi reached for his hand.

He drew back. "This is a free country, is it not?"

"Don't you try and turn the tables on me, pal. You have no business running around loose in a world you don't know anything about."

"So, I have no freedom, but you are free to laugh and fondle any man you choose."

"Fondle...what in Sam Hill are you talking about?"

"Hogan." Dominic all but spat out the word. "I saw you today, laughing with him, letting him hold you."

"It's not what you think, but so what if it was?"

"I do not like it. Or him."

"I'll alert the media."

"But obviously you like him. You like the way he stands so close to you, the way he puts his face so near yours when he speaks to you."

"Is that what all this is about? You're jealous?"

"No," he said, trying to hang on to his dignity. "Such emotion is beneath me." He knew she was right, and he wanted to shake her for it.

"The pavement's going to be beneath you in about three seconds, right after I deck you."

"Because I see the truth."

"No, because you're stupid," Remi told him. "And you're really making me mad, Dominic."

Now it was Dominic's turn to see red. "I believe, mistress," he said, his voice dripping ice, "the appropriate response would be, 'tough.'"

"Oh, oooh." She waved her finger at him. "You just stepped over the line, pal. You want to run and play? Fine. Go make a fool out of yourself. As far as I'm concerned, I can't get you out of my life fast enough." And she turned and stomped off into the darkness.

Dominic thought about going after her, then decided against it. He spun on his heel and started walking back toward the bar. Nay, he thought. She was the one flinging insults. She was the one acting like a shrew.

He stopped, running his hands through his hair in frustration.

He had treated her badly, and he knew it. All because he was jealous.

God's teeth, he wanted her so much he had let his rage get the upper hand. Angry at her for being right and himself for allowing his pride to rule his head, Dominic spun back around, intending to run after her.

And heard her scream.

# 8

"Remi!"

There were so many dark spots in the parking lot that for a second he couldn't find her. Panic, rage and desperation surged through his body.

"Remi!" he roared.

Then he heard a slap, a muffled scream and the sounds of a struggle coming from somewhere among the row of cars to his right.

"Remi, where are you? I'm—"

Another scream cut him off, and at the same time he saw her head pop up from between two parked cars.

The shadowy figure of a man jumped up behind her and grabbed her.

"Dominic," came Remi's hoarse screech as the man slammed her up against a car and attempted to strangle her.

A heartbeat later, the man's hands were gone, and she heard what sounded like a bone snapping in two. She spun around to see her attacker on the ground, Dominic on top of him, repeatedly bashing his fist into the man's face.

"Dominic! Oh, God, Dominic, stop!" Realizing he had no intention of stopping until the attacker was dead, she reached down and tried to pull him off. "Stop. You'll kill him."

Against his superior strength, her efforts were useless. Panicked that he would be the one hauled off to jail, she knew she either had to get some help, or find some way to make him stop. So, she got his attention the only way she knew how.

She filled her lungs with air and screamed as loud as she could.

"Remi?" Dominic's head snapped up, and the pounding of his fist stopped.

"Don't," she cried. "Don't kill him. He isn't worth it."

Dominic got to his feet, lifting her assailant partly off the pavement. Remi began to sob, and abruptly, he let the man drop back to the ground.

"Remi, Remi." He took her into his arms. "Are you wounded? Did he hurt you?"

"N-no. I.d-don't th-think so," she gasped, her entire body trembling.

Dominic released her, intending to finish off the brigand that had assaulted her. But when he turned back, the man had crawled some distance, risen on shaky legs and was making good his escape. Always the warrior, his first instinct was to go after the man.

"Please." Remi tugged on his arm. "Let him go."

"You beg for his life?" Dominic bellowed, confused. "He is vermin, not fit to—"

"No," she pleaded. "For yours. He might have a knife, or a gun. He could kill you. Please, please, don't chase him. Don't leave me alone."

Her last appeal got through to him when nothing else could have, and he ceased straining against her desperate hold.

"God's teeth, did he harm you?"

She shook her head.

"Are you certain? Should we seek a physician? If he has caused you harm, I will hunt him down like the worthless cur he is." Gently, he urged her several steps into the light.

A cursory examination of her face and neck revealed several bruises that would look worse by morning, but nothing more. He stared into her eyes, now glistening with tears and felt as if his heart had been ripped out of his body.

"I thought he . . ." Dominic folded her into his embrace, holding her tightly. "I thought you were . . ."

He couldn't finish his sentence because his mind refused to validate the image of that man brutalizing someone as delicate and precious as the woman in his arms. For all the knights he had faced in hand-to-hand combat, for all the bloody battles he had weathered, none had ever struck terror to his heart the way this encounter had.

"H-he came out of n-nowhere. It was s-so dark and I thought he had a knife. Dominic," she whispered, the adrenaline beginning to diminish, and with it, her strength. "Oh, Dominic, hold me. Just hold me."

"Aye, love," he promised.

Standing in that darkened parking lot, he could easily have held her until the sun came up. He could have kept her in his arms forever. But even forever wouldn't have been long enough to comfort her, to soothe her shattered confidence.

Finally, with a deep sigh, she drew back and looked into his face. "Take me home." Remi had never felt so fragile in her life. At that moment, her strongest wish was that he swoop her up into his arms and whisk her away to some private place where he could hold her through the night. The desire was irrational, born out of her fear . . . and powerful.

He looked at her car, then back at her. "Hell's fury. I cannot," he said, angry at himself at not being able to do the one thing she asked.

"It's okay." Smiling, she touched his cheek. "I guess I'm not really the damsel-in-distress type. Let's just go home."

On the journey to the condo, she said nothing, instead reaching for his hand each time she came to a stoplight. Outwardly she was calm, but he suspected she was barely holding herself together. Those suspicions were confirmed as soon as she was inside her own home. The calm dissolved into a puddle of tears.

"I-I've never been so terrified . . . At one point, I actually think I . . . I went weak in the knees."

Seeing her so distraught tore him apart. He wanted to rage at the heavens that she had been subjected to such an ordeal, and go down on bended knee to give thanks for her safety, all at the same time. Instead, he followed his instincts.

In one fluid motion, Dominic swept her into his arms and carried her upstairs. Without turning on the lights, he deposited her so gently on the bed, she could have been made of spun sugar. Her peace of mind, he knew, was almost as frail.

"Tell me what you wish and I will see to your comfort. Something I may fetch—"

"I-I'm cold," she said, her sobs beginning to quiet.

He took the quilt at the foot of her bed and spread it over her, tucking it in around her narrow shoulders. His own hands were shaking. "Better?"

Remi smiled shyly and murmured her thanks.

She looked like a helpless waif, her luminous eyes glistening from her recently shed tears. It broke his heart to see her so. He wanted to wrap her in his arms and never let her go, to shield her so that no harm would ever come to her again. To promise her all that he had, all that he was.

But he could not promise her his honor or his protection. How could he protect her from a century away? He could not make such a promise, and even if he could, there would be no time to keep it.

Gazing down at her, Dominic knew how much she needed comfort, and how vulnerable she was. Most of all, he knew he should leave her. Because if he stayed, he would take her in his arms and kiss her, and if he kissed her, he was not certain he could resist taking her. His body was almost shaking with the need to make her his. To love her mind, body and soul. Every noble instinct he had ever possessed cried out for him to leave. Every desire, every longing cried out for him to stay.

Plumbing the depth of strength he thought gone, he found just enough to do the noble thing.

"I..." He reached out a hand to stroke her hair, but stopped. "Sleep, my lady." The once-formal address was now an endearment on his lips. "You must rest. I will be downstairs." With one last tuck of the quilt, he rose and went to the door. "If you require anything, call out to me. Promise?"

"P-promise."

The instant he was gone, she wanted to call him back and beg him to stay with her, hold her until... Until forever?

*Yes.*

Even as she made the admission to herself, Remi knew she was asking for the impossible. But at the same time, she knew she wanted it. She wanted him.

And he had walked away.

She sat up in bed, staring at the empty doorway.

Surely he knew that she needed him. Hadn't she been the one to initiate the kiss in the pool? Was it possible all the emotion, all the desire was one-sided?

*No.*

She had seen the hunger in his eyes, seen his hands shake as he almost touched her. He wanted her, too. And he had to know she was willing. Yet he had walked away. Why?

*I never lie. Nor take unfair advantage, especially of a woman. My word is my honor...*

As she recalled the words he had spoken the first night they met, Remi realized that the twentieth century might have blown past the age of chivalry, but for Dominic, it was more than some long-ago concept. It was a part of this life. A part of his honor. Was it so unusual, then, for him to think he was taking unfair advantage of her? No. In fact, it made perfect sense.

*I would cut out my heart before I hurt you.*

*You should have a man who can give you the stability of heritage you deserve.*

Stability. Heritage. She thought about the bar sinister across his shield. He was the bastard son of the Duke of Kerwick, and she knew that in his time, such men had little or nothing they could claim as their own. No land or title, without which they were scarcely more than servants. Some, and she suspected Dominic to be among that group, found favor at court or were accorded great honor by virtue of their victories in battle. It was easy to understand how important stability and heritage would be to such a man. Such a man would undoubtedly forfeit his life rather than lose them.

Was that why he had walked away? Because he felt he had nothing to offer her?

Oh, but he did. He had something stable. Something so precious it renewed itself generation after generation.

"Just your heart," she whispered to the darkness. "What more could I ask?"

She couldn't help remembering staring at him across her desk that first night, trying to decide if this dashing man with the strange speech and bizarre tale was to be believed.

She had made that decision, in a heartbeat, knowing her course of action might prove wrong.

She decided to believe.

Now, just as quickly, she made another decision. And it too might prove wrong, but she didn't think so. Nothing had ever felt so right in her life.

She decided to trust her heart.

Remi scrambled from the bed, dashed across the room to her lingerie chest and opened one of the drawers. Carefully, she withdrew a robe that was more a cloud of silk than a garment. More seduction than substance.

DOMINIC KEPT telling himself that he had done the right thing, the noble thing. His head accepted it. His body did not. Stretched out on the futon, a rumpled sheet twisted around his body, he stared up at the ceiling. Days, he told himself, only a few days left. He could maintain control for that long.

*God's teeth, in a few days I will be dead from wanting her.*

"Dominic."

Her voice was so soft, at first he thought he had imagined her calling his name in the dark.

"Dominic?"

He sat up on the edge of the futon, and reached for the lamp.

"Don't turn on the light."

She was standing in the doorway to the living room, the faint glow from the streetlights outside outlining her body. The skirt and blouse she had been wearing when he put her on the bed had been exchanged for a robe that barely came to her knees and clung to her body the way he longed to do.

"I . . . I didn't thank you for rescuing me," she said. "You saved my life."

"Your gratitude is not necessary."

She came toward him, stopping beside his bed. Dominic's heart almost shot out of his body. A body already hard.

"Yes, it is necessary," she insisted. "I can only imagine what might have happened if you hadn't been there."

"I only regret that I did not arrive sooner. If I had not been so stubborn—"

"You?"

She sat down on the futon, not a foot away. The sound of softly rustling silk was almost like a whip against his skin. His breath wedged in his throat. He dared not touch her or he was lost.

"I did my fair share of acting like a mule tonight," she said. "When I dig in my heels, it takes an act of God and Congress to move me. And look what kind of trouble I caused."

Hearing her berate herself was painful. She was blameless. "Nay—"

"Yes. I had no business following you to Slim's. If I hadn't been acting like a jackass, none of this would have happened. It's all my fault."

"Nay. Never think it."

"You were right—"

"Nay!"

Then he made the fatal mistake of touching his finger to her mouth. And the truth poured out along with a stream of emotion that threatened to become a riptide.

"I was jealous." His fingertip skimmed across her bottom lip. "The thought of another man touching you sent me into a rage. I had no right to think of you as mine, but I did. God help me, I still do."

Remi's body trembled, less from her ordeal than from his touch. "He wasn't—" she could barely catch her breath, "—touching me. Not the way you thought. Clint means nothing to me. Less than nothing."

"Truly?"

"Truly," she said, her voice husky. "I told you there was no man in my life."

Dominic felt like a weight had suddenly been lifted from his shoulders. "Aye."

"It was true . . . then."

"And now?"

Remi knew what he was asking. She knew her answer could mean the difference between loving briefly and never loving at all. In the end, the answer was simple, and from her heart.

"You're in my life, Dominic."

"But I cannot—"

"Give me forever, I know. I'm not asking for it."

He took her hand, kissing her palm. "There are things about me that you do not—"

"I saw your shield."

Dominic's heart almost stopped beating. She knew his shame, yet she was here. "I can offer you nothing. No past. No future."

"I don't need tomorrow. I need today. I need you, for the next minute, the next hour. Whatever time we have. I want you to make love to me, Dominic."

"But time—"

"Is our enemy. Don't let it rob us of what we both want."

He knew he should deny her, for her own good. But how could he? How could he resist the siren song of his own heart?

"You are certain?"

"Yes. This is right."

He closed his eyes briefly, and when he opened them she saw overwhelming relief. She smiled. "Did you think I'd change my mind?"

"I prayed you would not. You have bewitched me."

"Have I? Maybe I'm a witch, after all."

"Sweet witch," he said, kissing each of her fingertips. "I have never wanted a maid as I do you." The intensity in his eyes was a visceral caress.

Sensations rippled through her like expanding rings of heat from a fire burning deep inside her. Slowly, she slipped her hand from his, and stood.

For one torturous second, he thought she intended to fly from him, but instead she untied the sash of the robe and pushed it from her shoulders.

And stood before him as God had made her, naked, beautiful.

She was breathtaking, a goddess. He reached out a hand and pulled her back down to the bed.

"I am under your spell," he said, running his fingertips from her neck, over her shoulder. Lifting her slender arm, he placed a string of kisses from the inside of her wrist upward, bringing her closer to him with each feather-light touch of his lips.

Remi went willingly, eagerly, her mouth finally meeting his in a deep kiss. She moaned as her breasts touched his chest. The heat from his body was like a fire branding her without burning. His heartbeat pounded wildly to match her own, and she shivered in his embrace as his hand caressed her naked back.

"Your skin tastes like nectar," he murmured as he kissed her shoulder, the hollow of the throat. His voice, his warm breath against her neck sent more heat cascading through her body. She allowed her head to fall back to expose the graceful arch of her throat to his searching mouth. It gave him greater access, but he wanted more. Almost leaning her over his arm, he bent his head and tasted her, his tongue licking the peak of first one breast, then the other.

Remi's breath broke on his name. She shivered again and sighed as his tongue circled her nipple then slowly drew it into his mouth. "Dominic," she whispered raggedly, her hand going to the back of his head, urging him not to stop.

Even as he told himself to temper his passion, his blood hammered in his loins, pushing the limit of his control. He had never felt so powerful and so helpless at the same time. And he had never known the depth of desire that literally shook him. He wanted, needed to be inside her body the way he needed his next breath.

"I...don't know what you like, what pleases you," she said as he lay her back on the bed.

Quickly removing his underwear, he stretched out beside her, letting her feel the strength of his desire. "You please me in every way."

"Can I . . . touch you?"

For all her boldness of a moment ago, she now seemed incredibly shy. "Aye, sweet witch. Wherever you please, whenever you please."

Slowly, Remi let her hand glide over his broad chest, his flat stomach to the ridge of his arousal. "So smooth," she whispered, surprised. "Like satin. Warm satin."

The astonishment in her voice should have alerted him, but he was too caught up in the haze of passion. Her delicate fingers stroked his length, driving him higher and higher and nothing mattered but the feel of her hand on him, her body next to his, waiting, willing.

Dominic's hands slid over her body, caressing her breasts, hips and thighs, coming at last to the warmth at the apex of her long silky legs. Gently, he drew her legs apart and caressed the nest of soft curls, then to the treasure they hid. Unerringly, his fingers parted her sleek petals and he stroked her slowly, drawing a shivering cry from her. The sound was a powerful aphrodisiac and his passion redoubled.

Instinctively, Remi arched her body, craving more of the wickedly delicious sensations his touch created. Another slow, gliding caress made fire shimmer through her. With each stroke her body tightened and her need intensified, spiraling upward to she knew not where.

"Open for me," he whispered against her mouth, then kissed her deeply, hotly.

She shifted, easing her legs farther apart, then moaned at the slow penetration of his fingertip. Again, forever, it seemed, he caressed her until her whole body was taut with need.

"Dominic, please..."

"Aye, love," he promised, settling himself between her slender legs even while he continued to stroke her sultry heat. He pressed forward, replacing his fingers with his turgid flesh, easing just inside her. Then back and forth, short sweet strokes, a prelude to joy, despite the passion that hammered at him for immediate release. Gradually, he pressed deeper and deeper until . . . he felt the veil of her virginity.

Dominic froze, sweat glistening on his body as he fought for control.

"Please," she begged when he hesitated, "don't stop."

"Remi—"

"No." With her hands on his hips, she arched her body into his, giving him no choice.

Dominic sheathed himself inside her in one long stroke, then held himself still. A heartbeat later, he began to move, rocking against her.

The instant of pain was overwhelmed by the waves of pleasure at being joined with him. As he rocked, she rose to meet him, a sweet, golden fire flowing through her body, building steadily. She writhed beneath him, twisting, begging for she knew not what, knowing only that he and he alone held the answer.

It came in a relentless, convulsing pleasure that burst inside her like the sun exploding.

Dominic felt her release and sought his own in her sweet fire. Together they burned, rose from the ashes and burned again.

"My LADY," he whispered, brushing a damp curl from her neck. "You are my lady."

"A very tired lady."

There was a long pause. "You should have told me."

Remi knew he was referring to the fact that she was a virgin. She snuggled closer. "I thought you knights went around deflowering virgins all the time. It's in all the romance novels."

When he didn't answer, she raised herself onto her elbow and looked into his handsome face. "Sorry, that wasn't funny, was it?"

"Nay. Not in the least."

She sighed. "I didn't tell you because I was afraid you would stop."

"As well I would have."

"Now, see, that's just my point—"

"Remi, I have taken a precious gift that should rightfully belong—"

"To the man I love?"

"Aye."

"It does."

Dominic gazed down into her beloved face. When had a woman ever been so giving, so loving? She granted him his heart's desire and made no demands, save giving him more pleasure. She offered herself totally and completely. No pretense, no defenses. He was humbled by her purity of spirit. By her love. And soon by her loss.

"You break my heart, sweet witch."

"Because I love you?"

"No, because I love you, and soon you'll be gone from me."

She ran her fingertip over his forehead, then slid her hand into his hair. "Then we should make every minute count. Every second."

"Aye," he agreed, allowing her to pull his head down for a long, wet kiss that had both of them needy and eager in moments.

"'Tis too soon, love," he said against her mouth. "You are not used to lovemaking."

"I can't think of a better way to get used to it." She reached up, closing her hand around his hard shaft.

"Sweet heaven," he said between clenched teeth. "You test my control."

"I don't want to test it. I want you to lose it."

In one swift motion he slipped his hands beneath her hips, lifting her. "My lady," he growled, planting himself deep inside her. "I am your servant."

# 9

REMI WAS LIVING in a dreamworld, and on borrowed time. She knew it, she just simply tried to ignore it. Easy enough to do when she could focus all her thoughts, as well as her attention, on Dominic. And focusing her attention on him was certainly no hardship.

They had made love long into the night. Sweet, wild, tender, ravenous love. And she had gloried in his every kiss, every touch. It was as if her body had been awakened from a long, cold sleep to brilliant sunshine and fresh air, sweet enough to taste. That was what he had done for her. He had given her a taste of life, real life.

When she thought of all the wonders she had seen in her travels with her parents, all the cultures she had experienced, they paled in comparison to the world Dominic had opened for her. He had painted the universe with the color of passion.

Strange, she thought, watching him groom his horse. She had lived her whole life in a Technicolor world, but it had taken a man from the Dark Ages to make her see the light of who she was, what she needed to be truly happy.

At the other end of the stable, Dominic patiently groomed Navarr. He brushed the stallion's neck, withers, back and rump until the animal's coat gleamed like polished ebony. Then he picked all four hooves clean. Finished, he stretched the muscles across his shoulders. Then, holding the bridle, he stroked the stallion's forehead as he looked into the horse's huge dark eyes.

"I wonder, brave fellow. Had you the power of speech, would you tell your master that he is less a master than a slave? A slave to the arms of a woman, to her lips, her warm, giving body." Navarr snorted, as if in disbelief.

"Aye. Me, a warrior who has faced death many times and lived to tell the tale. But it is the truth, old friend. This lady holds my heart captive. And on the fingers of one hand, I can count the days before she sets me free."

Navarr nuzzled his master, the velvety softness of his nose feeling almost like a caress against Dominic's neck. "But how can I be free without her? What good is time when I must spend it alone?" He stroked the horse's neck. "We are bound by our honor, you and I, to a life of service. You as a loyal steed, myself as a knight. But I tell you the truth. If you and I were the only ones that mattered, I would trade honor for love, and be glad of it."

"He's magnificent."

Dominic turned to find Remi standing on the other side of the stall door. "Aye. You should see him in battle. Truly, he is a warrior in his own right."

"I can believe it, looking at his chest, and those powerful legs." Her words were for the animal's beauty, but her eyes were on the man. He was himself a sleek animal, all power and muscle. She felt weak in the knees just looking at him.

"The two of you are a perfectly matched pair. I can just imagine you on a battlefield. You in your armor, proud and tall in the saddle. Navarr straining at the bit. Banners flying, trumpets sounding. Your enemies probably take one look at you guys, then turn tail and run."

He grinned. "I have yet to see many tails, but I will be certain to take notice when next I do battle."

And there would be a next battle, Remi thought. For him and for Navarr. The small voice of reason reminded her that soon they would return to the life they knew, and she would be left with only memories. Suddenly, she didn't want to be reminded. She wanted to pretend, at least for a while, that they had a future.

"Let's cook out tonight," she announced. "How would you like a nice, big, thick, juicy steak? Never mind," she added before he could answer. "You'll love it, trust me."

HE DID. In the privacy of her tiny backyard, Remi prepared a succulent piece of meat over an open fire contained in a metal drum she called a grill. The food was fresh and tasty, and by the end of the meal he was quite replete.

He helped her carry the plates and utensils into the kitchen, then they came back outside. Remi turned off the porch light as she closed the back door behind her.

The night was sultry, but he felt no inclination to be inside. Stars twinkled overhead as he reclined on a narrow piece of furniture that was neither bed nor couch, but some of both. Remi joined him, stretching out beside him, her leg thrown over his.

"What is this strange contraption?" He rolled onto his side to make more room for her.

"A chaise lounge, or just a lounger."

"An appropriate name." With his fingertip he stroked the line of her jaw, then gently ran his hand from her neck, down her arm, over her hip to the hem of her shorts. "I seem to want to do nothing but lounge." He slipped his hand beneath the shorts, caressing her thigh.

"Nothing? You're sure there's nothing better you'd like to do?"

"Possibly."

"I'm open to suggestions." She licked her slightly parted lips, drawing his hot-eyed gaze.

He was already hard, and watching her tongue glide over her lips did nothing to ease his discomfort. "I fear all my suggestions would require you to be naked."

"I can live with that," she said, a seductive smile on her lips as she rose from the lounger and led him inside.

Moments later they were in her bed, both gloriously naked and without need of any suggestions as to what to do. Each knew exactly what they wanted for themselves, and for each other.

Last night had been for deep, searing kisses and the wonder of discovery. Tonight, what began as playful hunger quickly escalated to raw, unadulterated passion.

The instant Dominic's mouth took possession of hers, Remi was thrown into a hot whirlwind of sensations, desire shimmering through her body. Somewhere in the back of her mind, the small voice she had been trying to deny reminded her that time was fleeting. The only real time was now. This second. This touch. This kiss. A feeling of urgency washed over her in wave after towering wave. And like Venus rising from the sea, she rose from the swirling imperative of her emotions to claim her need. Her mate.

Breathless with the heat of longing, she arched her body into his, letting him know how much she wanted him. How much she hungered for the surcease only he could give.

If Dominic had expected the sweet but willing virgin of the night before, he was pleasantly surprised. She was on fire for him. Almost as if she wanted to burn them up with her desire.

But he met her flame for flame. Her hunger fed his, and when he parted her legs and plunged into her silky heat, she welcomed him. Rocking against her, he tried to temper his passion, but he could not. Even if he had been able to slow his pace, she would not allow it. She was wild in his arms, rising to meet him thrust for thrust. Unable to resist her siren call, he stroked deeper, harder, until finally he felt her unravel beneath him. A heartbeat later, he followed her into the sweet, fiery abyss that burned, fused and melded them together, soul to soul.

THE FOLLOWING MORNING, Dominic watched as Remi busied herself preparing their breakfast. While strips of meat sizzled in a pan, she chattered away like a magpie. He knew what she was doing with this bright, pointless prattle. And if it would change anything, he would gladly have joined her, talking until the moon and stars fell from the sky. But they could not deny reality. And their reality was barely two days away. Time was running out.

"You know," she said, cracking eggs into a bowl and beating them furiously. "I was thinking that maybe you would like to have some real fun. We have this place called Six Flags Over Texas."

"Remi."

"It's like, uh . . ." She turned the bacon in one pan, lowering the heat, then poured the eggs into another. "Well, let's see, I guess the closest thing I could compare it to in your time would be a fair or feast." Her back was to him, and she didn't see him rise and come to her.

"Of course, we can't go during the day, but we could go some evening," she said, stirring the eggs.

"Six Flags is great at night. Or, some evening we could take a little ride. North Texas is noted for their ranches. Quarter horses, mostly. Up around Denton and Pilot Point. It's not far at all. You would love the land. It's perfect for raising horses and—"

His arms closed around her and he simply held her.

Remi held herself stiff in his arms for a moment, then her body sagged against him. The spatula slipped from her hand. She had no more words, no more energy to pretend.

"My beautiful enchantress." He bent his head and kissed her ear, her neck. He could not allow her to go on pretending, as wonderful as it was.

Damn him. He wasn't even going to let her have the satisfaction of imagining for only a little while. "I wish I were," she said on a ragged sigh, "I wish I had the power to . . ."

"To change history?"

"Yes."

"Would that it were so, my lady."

"You know, at first, I didn't like it when you called me mistress or my lady. But I've changed my mind."

"Have you, love?"

"Oh, yes."

"You are my lady, true and fair. If it were within my power, I would never leave you."

"But it's not. Your destiny will take you from me and there is nothing either of us can do about it."

"Nay. There is not."

"Then I guess we should get back to work on the chant."

"Aye."

Bacon and eggs forgotten, she turned in his arms and looked into his clear blue eyes. "Tonight, huh?" Her fingers skimmed up his chest to investigate the hollow at the base of his throat. She felt his pulse hammering.

His arms tightened, bringing her closer. "Tonight," he reiterated.

"And we need to really concentrate on making some progress."

"Absolutely."

"I mean, we need to keep our . . . urges in check."

"Aye, love."

"Think we can?" she asked, more than a little skeptical.

"I think," he said, kissing her eyelids, cheek, then her lips, "we must."

Looping her arms around his neck, Remi raised on tiptoe and kissed him deeply. He kissed her back just as thoroughly. And neither cared that their breakfast was burning or that they would probably be late for work.

ON THE DRIVE HOME that afternoon, they were less talkative than usual. Long silences stretched between them filled with the words neither wanted to hear, but each knew must be said.

Namely, that their time together could be counted in hours, not days.

"I'm not much in the mood to cook tonight," Remi told him. "So, you're about to get an introduction to fast food."

"Fast food?"

"Loaded with fat and calories." She whipped the Mustang into a fried-chicken restaurant and drive-thru. "You'll love it. Trust me."

In minutes they drove out with chicken, potato salad and bread. "Amazing," Dominic said, inhaling the delicious aromas filling the car. "I like this."

"You ain't seen nothing yet."

By the time they arrived at her condo, they had added dessert to their stash of food. Again, to Dominic's amazement, from another drive-thru.

"And this is called frozen yogurt?" he asked, taking his first bite of a flavor she had informed him was double chocolate fudge.

"Like it?"

"Aye. It tastes like a cold pudding. Delicious." He glanced over at hers. "Why is yours different?"

"Because mine's called peach parfait. Wanna bite?"

"Aye."

"We'll trade. You give me some of yours, and I'll give you some of mine. Deal?"

"Deal," he echoed.

They prolonged eating their treat, but finally, they'd run out of dessert and excuses.

"Remi—"

"I know," she said reluctantly, wanting to curse the very thing she loved most about him. His sense of responsibility. "We've got work to do."

"Aye."

Dominic rose from the table, and held out his hand. Remi took it, and together they went into the living room to continue their search for the chant that would send him back. They worked quietly, until some time near midnight Remi said softly, "I think I found it."

Dominic looked up from his work at the opposite end of the couch. "How can you be certain?"

"Because the words and translations match closer than any we've come across. And because we've run out of chants, at least the good ones, as far as I can tell. Look for yourself," she said, and passed him the book, along with her dictionary. She leaned back against the sofa and closed her eyes.

"It would seem so," he agreed after reading the translations.

"We have to wait for the right time."

"The day after tomorrow."

"Yes. Since the history book stated that you reappeared on that date, we dare not jump the gun or it might prove..." She didn't want to say disastrous, didn't even want to think it. "It might complicate things. We have two shows, a matinee and an evening performance. I think we should...should aim for the matinee. That way, if anything goes wrong—"

"You expect difficulties?"

"No, but we're going to have to concentrate, and try to duplicate the exact conditions of the night you came forward. Everything may go off without a hitch the first time. If . . . if not, then the matinee will just be a dry run for the evening performance."

"So," he said, hesitant to meet her gaze for fear of seeing his own pain reflected there. "We have succeeded."

"Yeah? Then why do I feel like I've just signed your death warrant?"

The pain in her voice filled the room like a living, hurting presence. He knew it, recognized it like an old friend. Quickly setting the books aside, he pulled her into his embrace.

"It's not fair," she whispered.

"Nay, love. 'Tis not. But we are powerless to change it. Each of us must do what we know is right."

Remi clutched at his T-shirt. "What's right is loving you. Hold me, Dominic. Hold me tight." *And never let me go.*

He did. All through the night.

BREAKFAST THE NEXT morning was an unenthusiastic, reluctant affair with neither of them able to keep up even a pretense of brightness. Unfortunately, the workday was not so reluctant. It passed in a blur, interrupted only by the moments when one of them would look up to find the other a short distance away with a warm smile, a yearning glance.

Neither had much of an appetite after work, and Remi suggested they raid the refrigerator and just "graze."

"Mistress," Dominic had said in mock indignation. "Do you take me for a bovine?"

When Remi laughed at his remark, it tore at Dominic's heart. It had been the only time during the entire day that her smile had reached her eyes. After grazing on crackers, cheese, fruit and more frozen yogurt, they went into Remi's office.

"Sit here." She patted the seat of an extra chair she had pulled up next to her computer, which was already on and opened to an empty file. "We need to get the events of the night you came forward in order. Before, during and after. Everything we can remember, even the smallest detail. Let's start with what was happening before you heard—didn't you say a voice?"

"Your voice," he reminded her, his own deep, husky and seductive.

Remi turned to gaze into his eyes. "Have you wondered why, out of all the men doing battle that day, I called to you, and not some other knight?"

"Aye. I thought it strange then, even stranger now. But I alone heard your voice, even though my squire was nearby. At first I thought perchance a woman had wandered onto the battlefield and had been wounded."

"Why?"

He thought for a moment. "Because your call sounded most . . ." He struggled for the right word, right phrase.

"Urgent?"

"Not so urgent, as from the heart. Aye, that is it. Your call was from deep within your heart, your soul."

"For a hero," she whispered. "My knight in shining armor. Slayer of dragons, rescuer of damsels in distress."

"I am but a man, my love. Not a hero."

"You're my hero. And you will be one to all of England when you save the king."

"Would that I could forfeit that honor for time in your arms."

"I know," she said, desperately trying to keep the promise she had made to herself not to cry. "What will you do when you return? I mean, what kind of life will you live? Will you always be a warrior?"

"My life will be as before, for it is the only one I know. The only one I thought possible until now."

"But soon the wars will be over and you won't have to fight anymore. Will you . . . will you marry someday?"

"In the past, I thought marriage was for land and heirs."

"And now?"

"Now I know that there should be a bond between a man and a woman, not just a contract. How could I settle for less now that I have known the joy of this bond, this love I thought beyond my reach?"

Remi lost the battle against her tears, as they slid down her cheeks. Gently, Dominic brushed them away.

"Do not cry, love, I beg you."

"I can't help it." She sniffed, reaching for a tissue. "I'm okay, really." She wiped her face and squared her shoulders.

"So brave."

"No, just realistic." She pushed her wayward hair from her face, and pulled herself together. "We have to finish this."

They worked for almost two hours until they had every detail they could remember noted and in the right sequence. If they followed this outline exactly, recited the chant correctly...and prayed, Dominic should be back in his own time within fifteen or sixteen hours.

Hours, Remi thought as she watched Dominic read the three double-spaced pages of details she had printed out. He would be gone in only hours. She felt as if she were waiting to be handed a death sentence. How could she bear it? The thought of years stretching out before her without him was almost unthinkable. No matter what century he came from, Dominic was the man she had waited for all her life. How could she exist without him?

As she had done twice since meeting him, she made a lightning-fast decision. She couldn't live without him, so the only solution was to live with him, regardless of where or when he lived.

She would go back with him.

The solution was so simple, Remi was amazed she hadn't thought of it before. And it wasn't as if she would be leaving behind the best job in the world, or a close-knit, loving family, for that matter. Of course, she would miss her parents, but they had each other, just as they always had. As long as they were together, they would be fine.

For the first time in her life, Remi understood the bond her parents shared. As a child, she had never quite been able to comprehend the kind of love that was so special, so all-consuming that it barely made room for the children of such a union. Now she did. Now she saw it clearly.

Yes, she would miss her parents, but they would go on and be more than fine. They would be wonderful. As for her brother, Mark, she would miss him dreadfully, but perhaps someday he would meet someone and understand her decision.

And she didn't delude herself that she would be a fairy princess going back to her fairy-tale kingdom. She would be giving up everything she took for granted on a daily basis, including modern medicine and creature comforts. But she didn't care. Living without Dominic would be the real hardship.

She knew he would resist, but she was determined to stick to her guns. She was going and that was that.

At last, Dominic set aside the pages. "I believe we are ready."

"Yes," she said, knowing her decision was right.

They climbed the stairs together.

"Dominic," she said once they were in bed. "I have something I want to tell you." She expected him to refuse, possibly even to get angry. He was, after all, one of the most passionate men she had ever known and that kind of passion rarely excluded anger.

"I want you to know that I've been happier in the short time we've been together than I can remember. Ever."

"'Tis the same with me."

"No, Dominic, I mean it. My childhood wasn't the greatest and you know firsthand that my love life hasn't been, well, it just hasn't been. When I'm with you, I feel alive in a way I've never experienced before. I don't want to give that up. I won't." She took a deep breath and said straight out, "I want to go with you."

He kissed her tenderly. "I thank you, but nay, love. I cannot allow it."

"But I love you."

"And I you, but I cannot ask you to give up your life here for one of hardship and uncertainty." What he did not tell her was that when he thought of his life past his return, past saving the king, he felt only a void where the rest of his life should be. It was possible that he, himself, did not survive the assassination attempt. How could he leave Remi in a world she did not know, in a time that was not hers?

"Dominic, I want to go. And what do you mean, you 'cannot allow it'?"

"Remi, you have no idea what life in my time is like. 'Tis hard. Doubly so on women. You would be giving up everything. It would kill me to see you in a life that amounts to scarcely more than servitude. I cannot let you do it."

She had been so prepared for his anger, she hadn't taken her own into account. "Excuse me, but just because I love you doesn't make me your property. I intend to take at least that much of my century back with me."

"You cannot go."

"Watch me." She scrambled from the bed, not sure where she was headed. Basically, anywhere but here. Expected or not, his rejection hurt like hell.

Dominic caught her before she reached the door.

"Do you think I do not *want* you with me?"

"It crossed my mind," she said, looking for an easy out.

"Do you think I would not give my life to have you with me? Do you? Look at me," he growled.

With his hands gripping her upper arms, he almost lifted her off the floor. "Are these the eyes of a man rushing to be free of you? Are these the arms of a man seeking to hold another?" He drew her higher and closer, moonlight from the bedroom window casting his face in shadow. "Are these the lips of a man who would have another's kisses once he had tasted yours?"

"Dominic, please." If begging was the only way, she would take it.

He yanked her into his embrace. "*Do not beg.* Anything but that."

She shivered, feeling the passion of his anger radiate through her body as he slowly let her slide down his body until her feet touched the floor.

"Is it possible you do not know that leaving you is tearing me apart? God's teeth, you have my heart, my soul. What is there left of me to return?"

"Then, let me—"

"Nay! You force me to tell you things I hoped to keep from you."

"What things? What *things* could be important enough to keep us apart?"

"You said there was no mention of me after August 29, 1485."

"Yes, but—"

"What if I did not survive the assassination attempt?"

The question made her blood run cold. *No . . . no.* She had never considered the possibility that he might not live.

"It is possible. Even probable that I could save Henry's life, yet lose my own. What would become of you then, my love? You would be alone in an unfamiliar time. And I would never forgive myself if I left you alone and unprotected."

He clasped both her hands in his and brought them to his lips. "I would haunt the moors for eternity with my pain.

"Even if I did survive, you know my position. It has not changed, nor will it. I can offer you nothing. No land, no home, no title. Nothing."

"Your love."

"Aye. You have that. You will always have it." He framed her face with his hands.

The plea in his voice stunned her, and she realized that he was speaking as Sir Dominic William Longmont, fifteenth-century knight of the realm. In his time, there could be no other way, no other life, but the one allotted him. It was one thing for a man to make the best of a bastard's life, another to ask a wife to share it with him. He was trying to spare her.

For the first time, she saw it from his perspective and realized that what she had asked was incredibly selfish.

"But Dominic—"

"No, sweet witch." He silenced her with a tender kiss as he took her into his arms, holding her close.

"No matter how much we love," he said, "it cannot be. In your heart, I know you understand."

After a long silence, Remi said softly, "I understand. I hate it, but I understand."

"Earlier you asked if I would marry. I did not answer."

"It's . . . it's okay. I . . . you have to go on—"

"There will be no other for me. You are my own true love, and I will have no other to wife."

"Oh, Dominic, no," Remi said, torn between being happy that he would never love anyone as he loved her, and sad because it would mean a lonely existence for him. "You should live a full, rich life. I want you to be happy. I don't want you to be alone."

"I will not be alone. Time will never truly part us. You will always be with me—" he touched his heart "—here."

With her tears again wetting her cheeks, she took his hand and, holding it in hers, she placed it over her heart. "And you will always be part of me. Always."

He gazed at the ring his mother had given him, a symbol of her love for him. He removed it from his little finger. "I pledge my love and devotion. Now. And for all time," he vowed, slipping the ring onto the third finger of her left hand.

Through tear-blurred vision, she looked down at the intricate silver band and the exquisitely carved falcon's head. She moved her hand ever so slightly and the ring glistened in the moonlight. "And I pledge my love and devotion. Enough to reach across time. Enough to last forever."

They made love, but not urgently as might have befitted their desperate circumstances, but rather, torturously slow. As if they could prolong time with each languid kiss, each maddeningly deliberate touch. Each soft stroke.

They whispered love words, and promises to remember, to hold close in his past, her future. Through the achingly brief night, they tried to love enough for two lifetimes.

# 10

THEY HAD GONE over the sequence of events so many times Remi thought she'd be able to recite them in her sleep. Still, they couldn't afford to make any mistakes.

When the moment arrived to call for the Black Knight, Remi would reverse her original call before speaking the chant. She fully expected her fellow actors to complain about her messing up her lines, but it couldn't be helped. Besides, taking a little heat would be the least of her worries once Dominic was gone.

Mentally, she went over the details again. She had given Tina, the actress who regularly played the sorceress, the day off with pay. She had also asked Paul Tinsdale, who portrayed the Black Knight, to wait several extra seconds before entering, telling him she felt it would heighten the suspense. In a few days, personnel would probably be screaming bloody murder. Remi didn't care. In a few days, she wouldn't care about anything except the fact that the man she loved would be out of her reach forever.

After having snuck Dominic's armor, shield and sword into her office, she helped him dress. Then, he returned the favor.

"It seems years ago that I assisted you out of this costume," he said, tugging her zipper into place.

"It does feel like a lot of time has passed since then," she agreed. Turning to face him, Remi squared her shoulders. "Time. I'm beginning to really hate that word."

"Have you the Druid book?"

She patted her pocket. "Right here. Along with my trusty magic wand and crystal ball conveniently stowed away in my sleeves. We've only got a couple of seconds to pull this off before Paul makes his entrance. Now remember, the actors will already be fighting when you enter the arena, so be careful."

"And Navarr?"

"I sweet-talked Tim into having him ready."

"Sweet-talk? What kind of sweet-talk?"

Remi took a deep breath, smoothing the folds of her skirt. "Just a little eyelash batting, some ego stroking and— What?"

Dominic was staring at her breasts, which seemed to be eager to escape the bounds of her snug-fitting costume. "Sweet witch, you tempt me even now."

"It's a little tight, isn't it?"

"Deliciously so."

"Well," she said, trying to be the brave woman he thought her to be, "at least your last image of me will be memorable."

He slipped his hand around her neck, urging her closer. "All my images of you are memorable. Some more so than others. But all are burned into my mind and heart."

They had said their goodbyes last night, along with whispered vows and lingering kisses. Now, there were only minutes left, each tick of the clock moving them closer and closer to the final separation.

"I love you," Remi said. "With all my heart and soul. Forever."

Dominic lifted her left hand and kissed the ring he had placed on her finger. "Before God, you are my true mate for this life and the next." He dipped his head, but before his lips could take hers, there was a knock on the door.

"Five minutes, Miz Balfour," Andy Collins announced through the door.

"Thanks," Remi called out, again fussing with her skirt, this time as a way to hide the fact that her hands were trembling.

One last, long kiss, then Dominic took her hand in his. "We must go."

At the entrance to the arena, Navarr was ready and waiting. Dominic mounted the huge war-horse, glancing down as Remi touched his foot in the stirrup on her way into the darkened arena. He reached down to clasp her hand, but she was already gone.

Remi took her place and waited, her nerves stretched to the breaking point. Dominic's very life might hinge on whether or not she said the right words at the right moment.

Offering up a quick prayer, she stepped up on the platform as music filled the darkness. She jumped at the blare of the trumpets, with barely enough time to settle down before the single spotlight illuminated her position. A murmur went through the audience as usual.

Arms outstretched, she turned in a circle, the faux gemstones on her cloak winking in the light. She folded her arms across her chest, tucking her hands inside the sleeves of her costume. Music swelled, trumpets blared and cymbals crashed. Then, in a sweeping gesture, she lifted her hands, a glistening crystal ball in one, a lighted wand in the other. Her platform rose from the arena floor as if by magic. As expected, the crowd cheered and applauded.

With a wave of her hand, she pointed to her right and the spotlight fell on four mounted knights. A similar gesture and the spotlight fell on four more mounted knights to her left. And while the audience's attention was focused on the knights, she tucked the wand back inside its hiding place.

Then, with trembling hands, she pulled the book of chants from her pocket. Already marked with a paper clip, she ran her fingernail to the spot, flipped it open and began her dialogue. When she reached the part to be reversed, she paused. Taking a deep breath, she swallowed hard and licked her lips, her nerves jangling like a falcon's jesses.

"I must have a great and valiant knight to champion the cause," Remi told her audience. "One courageous knight. A bold hero. Oh, ancient ones...return him."

As Remi lifted the glowing crystal ball above her head, signaling the beginning of the special-effects lightning, out of the corner of her eye she glimpsed Dominic entering the arena.

"Hear...hear me, valiant knight, as I speak the ancient words to send you home."

Fake lightning slashed across the arena, accompanied by pyrotechnics as she began to read the chant.

The bizarre-sounding but melodic words drifted over the audience as Dominic galloped toward the thick cloud of smoke that appeared to rise mysteriously from the floor of the arena.

Remi finished the chant just as Dominic vanished in the smoke. A second later, Paul Tinsdale appeared as scheduled.

But something was wrong.

She could feel it.

Or rather, not feel it. The vibrations she had experienced the night Dominic came forward were missing. Her body didn't tingle. And worse, the eerie blaze of blue-white lightning had never appeared.

She made her exit, gathered up her voluminous skirts and raced around to the staging area. Her heart in her throat, she rounded the corner... and ran full tilt into Dominic.

FOR SEVERAL SECONDS after they were safely behind the closed door to Remi's office, neither moved. They

simply stared at each other. Then they seemed to realize simultaneously that a few feet, not centuries,
separated them. Dominic pitched his helmet into a
chair and opened his arms, barely a second before she
flew into them, despite armor and chain mail.

"I knew something was wrong," she said, covering
his face with kisses. "I could feel it."

"Aye, it was not the same." He captured her lips for
a deep kiss.

When they came up for air, they simply held on to
each other, unsure of what to do next.

"We must discover our mistake," Dominic said,
putting an end to the pipe dream of a reprieve. "There
is but one more chance."

Remi sighed, her hand resting on his armored chest.
"I know. We've got three hours before the next show
to find out what went wrong."

"We must have forgotten a detail or perhaps we had
the wrong chant."

"I don't think it was the chant. Besides, there aren't
any more. We've been through them all. Lord, but we
went over every word, every movement, every...
thing. What in Sam Hill did we miss?"

"We will find it, love," Dominic assured her as he
began to remove his armor. "We must."

Two hours later, his certainty had diminished.

"It's got to be the storm." Remi pushed back her hair
in frustration. "That has to be the answer."

"Perhaps."

"What else could it be?"

"Truthfully, my love, at this moment, I could almost wish you were a sorceress. I fear that may be the only way we will find our answer. Time grows short."

"It's something we've overlooked," she said. "Something we thought so insignificant that it didn't matter." She threw up her hands in a gesture of frustration. "We just have to physically go through the whole thing, step by step. It's grasping at straws, but what the hell."

And so, with Dominic on one side of her office pretending it was a battlefield, and Remi on the other side pretending she was in the arena, they played out the fateful night scene by scene. But they found nothing out of sequence, discovered nothing had been omitted.

"We have forgotten something vital," Dominic insisted. "Some subtlety or nuance. Perhaps the tone in my voice, or yours."

"This is insane. My brain feels like it's turned to cold oatmeal. We've covered every moment, practically every second from the time I came into the arena and we're no closer than we were the day we started."

Dominic thought about that day. Thought about what happened to him *before* the battle and could find nothing of significance. "What did you do before you entered the arena?"

"Before?" Remi shrugged. "I put on my costume."

"Then what?"

"I waited until it was time for my entrance."

"Where did you wait?"

"In my office." She now picked up on the direction of his questions. "At the window. The storm was really getting ugly and I closed the blinds. Then Andy brought me the package with Mark's gift—the books—inside. I opened the box and took out the books . . ."

Her voice trailed off then her eyes widened. "That's it!" Remi cried. "I had two books that night. Mark sent me two old books for my birthday. The Druid one, and another, uh . . ." She paced in front of her desk, trying to remember. "Something about rogues. Rogues for all time. Rogues, rogues . . ." She stopped pacing. "No!" she said with a snap of her fingers. "*Rogues Across Time.* And I had it with me . . . the Druid book was on top of the other one."

"I do not understand—"

"I remember holding that book in my hand. And I remember getting some real weird vibes, but I just thought . . ." Her eyes wide, she glanced up at Dominic.

"What is it, love?"

"You."

"Me?"

"He looked a lot like you, or you looked like him. Anyway, I remember thinking that you resembled the knight in the book. Coincidence?" She shook her head. "I don't think so."

"Where is this book?" Dominic asked, still not sure she had found the missing piece to their puzzle.

"I didn't take it home, so it has to be here." Remi glanced around. "The drawer." She dashed around the corner of her desk and yanked open the top drawer.

And there it was.

Carefully, she lifted it out. "All along, we thought the chants were responsible, but maybe it was the chants *plus* this book."

The weird vibes Remi remembered were just as potent as the first time. "I can feel *something* when I hold it." She held the book out to him.

As soon as Dominic touched it, their joint reaction was swift and stunning. Suddenly, the air crackled with electricity and their bodies tingled as if the current was zinging through their blood.

"Aye," Dominic whispered, suitably awed.

Slowly, they lowered it to her desk and let go.

Remi reached out to open the book, then drew back her hand. "Now I'm almost afraid to touch it."

"With good cause."

Gingerly, she opened the weathered volume and flipped through the pages until she found the etching of the knight. "There." She pointed to the page.

Stepping around to peer over her shoulder, Dominic looked down at the drawing and was startled to see a definite likeness of himself. At the bottom of the page was a brief paragraph in very small type.

Remi read it out loud. "'Sir Dominic William Longmont was a knight of the realm and vassal to the Duke of Kerwick. As a warrior of uncommon bravery during the last battles of the Wars of the Roses In

1485, he supported Henry Tudor's claim to the throne of England. Longmont was the leader of a valiant but ill-fated force separated from the main battle at Bosworth Field. He survived and was later instrumental in saving the life of Henry the Seventh.'

"This is it," she said. "This is how you came and how you'll return. We've been looking in the wrong book all along. The Druid book was on top of this one. It never occurred to me that what brought you here was anything other than one of the chants." She looked into Dominic's eyes. "This time it will work. You'll . . . you'll go back."

"Aye, love."

A half hour later, the evening performance of Swords and Shields began as usual. The audience thoroughly enjoyed the show. They never realized that the actress playing the sorceress had changed some of her lines. They paid little, if any, attention to the armored knight astride a war-horse riding into a wall of manufactured smoke as the mock battle began. They never knew that two lives had been altered forever in that brief moment.

Clutching the volume of *Rogues Across Time* to her, Remi left the arena after her part in the performance, but she didn't run back to the staging area. There was no need. She knew there was no one there.

In her arms, the book was cold and still. As lifeless as her dream of happiness.

# 11

*The Past*

HE WAS HOME.

In body, at least, Dominic thought. He had left his heart centuries in the future.

Had it been only moments ago when he rode through the smoke, leaving Remi behind? Already it felt as if they had been parted for years. With a weary sigh, he turned his attention to the task at hand. Namely, finding the new king before the assassins did.

He had returned to the same battlefield from whence he'd left, but the battle and the warriors were no more. The battlefield was silent in the growing dusk. Not so, Kerwick Castle.

As Dominic and Navarr approached, the castle fairly hummed with activity. An unusual state for an hour when the servants should have been preparing for the night. Anxious to warn the king, Dominic rode straight into the bailey and dismounted.

"Lord Dominic!"

Glancing to his right, Dominic was taken aback to see his squire, Erik, come rushing up to greet him.

"God be praised!" the lad said. "We thought you dead."

"And I you." Smiling, Dominic clasped the young man's shoulders, giving them an affectionate shake. "And I you."

"I was most fortunate to have been struck on the head and left for dead," he said, clearly overjoyed to see his fierce lord again. "When they came to collect the bodies, they found me. We searched for you after the battle, but there were so many, and most . . ." Erik hesitated, as if recalling the sight of mangled bodies.

"Enough said, lad. 'Tis the way of war. There is apology in your voice when there should be none. The living must do just that. Live."

"Bless you, lord."

"Tell me, the Lady Alise, how does she fare?"

"Well, my lord. 'Twas she who found and healed me. She is truly blessed by God. Shall I fetch her, lord? She will be so happy to see you, and there is such news—"

"Hold fast. First tell me, is the duke in the keep?"

"Nay, lord," Erik said, taking Navarr's reins. "He and some knights, accompanied by men at arms, have ridden forth to meet the king."

"King Henry? He comes here?"

"Aye, lord, in honor of all that the duke did to help set the Tudor on the throne. There is to be a great feast. We have been preparing for over a week. Roast pig and hens, meat pies, mountains of food. But the hour grows late. They should have returned."

"Which road, lad? Which road do they travel?"

"The cart road from Redmore, lord."

"Listen well. Tell the captain of the guard a rider came with a message. Say he is to leave enough men to protect the keep and come *immediately* with the rest. And hurry, lad. The king's life may depend upon it."

Dominic grabbed Navarr's reins, vaulted onto the stallion's back and rode furiously out of the bailey.

Now that the wars were over and Henry had been enthroned, there was little reason to assign a full complement of guards for a royal procession. What better chance for brigands to carry out their deadly plan? And since the information from the history book had only given the date, not the circumstances, this most certainly had the earmarks of an opportune moment. As darkness approached, Dominic rode cross-country, pushing Navarr to his limit, all the while praying he would be in time.

He had no concept of how long he had ridden as he came upon a bend in the road and heard the sounds of battle: men shouting, steel clashing.

*God's teeth. I am too late!*

Coming upon the scene, his worst fears were confirmed. His father's men and the king's guards were engaged in battling a band of thirty or more attackers. Steel rang on steel, men shouted and cursed, horses snorted and whinnied as the struggle surged back and forth. And blood gleamed blackly under the rising moon.

Immediately, Dominic saw that the attackers had managed to separate the king from his guards. The only thing standing between the assassins and Henry the Seventh was his father, the Duke of Kerwick. Instantly, he realized the duke was no match for the cutthroats surrounding him. Heedless of his own safety, Dominic plunged headlong into the fray, wielding his sword like a madman. With shield and sword he fought his way toward the two cornered men.

"Dominic!" Kerwick shouted at seeing the son he thought dead.

"Hold fast," Dominic called as Navarr charged, sending chunks of dirt and grass flying under his thundering hooves. But as he drew near the duke and the king, a knight separated himself from the fighting and galloped straight at him.

Only Navarr's quick response to his command to turn and his raised shield prevented a fatal wound, as the brigand knight's sword came crashing down. Both war-horses staggered, then recovered.

Again, the knight swung his sword, again Dominic deflected the blow. And again, then yet again.

Brave knights fought all around him and the battle began to sway in the defenders' favor. But quick glances in the direction of the cornered king and duke, told Dominic time was short. His father fought valiantly, but his strength had lessened with age.

Thinking his foe distracted, the enemy knight raised his sword to make a two-handed swing intended to slice Dominic in half, but he hesitated a second too long. Standing in the saddle, Dominic swung, his sword gleaming in the moonlight as it made a fierce arc down and across the knight's chest, unhorsing the brigand with a fatal blow.

Now Dominic hewed through the attackers, swinging his sword as Navarr's powerful body helped make way. He showed no mercy as he drove relentlessly forward until at last, he was only scant yards from his father and the king.

As the duke looked up, catching sight of his warrior son, for half a heartbeat Dominic thought he saw the other man smile. Then, out of the darkness, one of the enemy knights bolted from a nearby stand of trees and was almost instantly upon the king. The attacker's battle-ax whistled through the air as he swung it over his head. With a touch of Dominic's heel to Navarr's flank, the powerful war-horse made a mighty lunge forward at the same time his master's sword deflected the ax's blow.

But the deflected blade found an unintended target. It glanced off the neck guard of William, Duke of Kerwick's armor and struck the high part of his shoulder. The duke slumped and fell from his charger.

Dominic's fury knew no bounds and he cut down the brigand like ripe wheat.

"Your Grace," Dominic gasped, coming quickly to his father's side.

To his credit, the king sprang from his horse, sword drawn in defense of his friend. However, the assassins had obviously seen that the tide of battle had turned, and were now making good their escape.

"Dominic," William whispered. "I thought 'twas a vision conjured from my grief. Is it truly you?"

"Aye. Save your strength, Your Grace."

"Alise...you must tell..." Kerwick's words trailed off and he passed out.

"Is he dead?" the king asked.

"No, Your Majesty, but he will be if we cannot staunch the flow of blood." Dominic glanced up at Henry's horse, blanketed with the emblems of England and St. George embroidered on silk. He pointed to the elaborate blankets. "With all due respect, Your Majesty—"

"You need not ask." At the king's command, the blankets were removed and used to stop the duke's bleeding.

"WHY HAVE WE HEARD nothing?" Dominic asked several hours later as he waited with his mother for word of his father's condition.

The king himself had been with the duke since the weary but victorious knights had arrived, bearing their lord home.

"We must pray," she said softly.

"Is there nothing else to be done? I do not belittle prayer, but God's teeth, surely—"

The massive oak door to Kerwick's chambers swung open and the king appeared.

Dominic bowed.

"Your Majesty," Lady Alise said, stepping into a deep curtsy.

"Nay, lady. I waive formalities where friends are concerned. And your husband is my true friend."

Dominic whipped around to face his mother. "Husband?"

"Aye, they were joined only three days ago," the king announced. "And I am happy to add that they will have many more years together."

With a rustle of silk skirts, Alise Longmont, Duchess of Kerwick, hurried forward and kissed Henry's hand. "Thank God, Your Majesty, thank God."

"As indeed we all should, but first, I want to thank your son."

Henry looked straight at Dominic. "You have done your country a great service this day. We are in your debt."

"I am your servant, as always, Your Majesty. No more. No less."

"What you have done goes far beyond mere service, Dominic Longmont. Later, you and I will talk of your future. Such a loyal servant should have lands and a title to pass on to his heirs."

Surprised, Dominic bowed to his sovereign. "Your Majesty's generosity overwhelms me."

"We are pleased. And now, Duchess," he said, smiling. "I think the best medicine for your husband would be to see your beautiful face." He turned to Dominic. "Come."

With his mother on the king's arm, Dominic followed behind as the three entered the candlelit chambers.

The Duke of Kerwick, wan and pale, was in his bed, propped up on pillows. A dark red stain indicated blood still seeped from the near-fatal wound on his shoulder.

"Alise." William held out his hand.

To Dominic's surprise, his mother raced forward, throwing herself on Kerwick's good side and bursting into tears. He had never seen his mother cry and the emotional display unsettled him. And dredged up painful memories.

He could not help remembering holding Remi in his arms while she cried on their last night together. The memory was bittersweet and pierced his heart with longing. Then his father called his name.

"Aye, Your Grace." He knelt on the other side of the bed. "I am here."

"I owe you my life."

"Nay, Your Grace. I have pledged you my honor, my—"

"'Tis your forgiveness I seek."

Dominic stared at the man who had sired him, yet who had addressed him directly no more than a handful of times in his whole life and wondered if the duke's injuries were far worse than suspected.

"I believed an untruth years ago." William turned to look at his wife and took her hand. "And because I was too young and too full of self-pride to trust my own heart, an injustice was done."

He turned back to Dominic. "To you and to your mother. Dominic, before God and your sovereign, I swear that you are my true son and heir. My only regret is that I waited so long to name you."

Stunned, Dominic glanced from his father to his mother. He had never seen such happiness shining in her eyes, such joy and even . . . peace. "I . . . I am at a loss for words, Your Grace—"

"You are a man fully grown and have your own life, but my fervent hope is that you will take your rightful, and well-deserved, place at my side." William, Duke of Kerwick, stretched out his pale hand and Dominic grasped it firmly. It was then he noticed the ring on the duke's left hand. A duplicate of the one his mother had given him and he in turn had given Remi, only larger.

"You do me a great honor, Your Grace."

"Nay, 'tis I that am honored, my son." Then, as if those words, so long in coming, had drained his energy, he lay back on the pillows and sighed.

"Now," the duchess said, rising. "You must rest, my love, and regain your strength." She brushed a lock of dark hair streaked with silver from the duke's forehead. The touch was so endearing, so achingly affectionate that Dominic wanted to cry out with the sweetness of it.

He got to his feet, discovering they were not as steady as when he'd entered the chambers. "Mother speaks with your best interest at heart, sir. And I can tell you from experience that she is a formidable healer when she is determined that her patient is to be put right."

"Aye." William gazed lovingly into Alise's eyes. "She is a rare woman, indeed."

"We will see how rare you think me on the morrow when I insist you drink the physician's potion."

"I will bid you good night, then." Dominic bowed to the king. "By your leave, Your Majesty."

When he left the chambers, his mother was still holding his father's hand.

A short time later, standing on the battlements, Dominic looked out over the land he had called home since he was a boy. Until a week ago, this was all he had known.

But it had never been all he wanted to know. Even as a child, he had been curious about other places, other people, other cultures. Perhaps it was because he had never felt as if he belonged at Kerwick. Perhaps it was because the one thing he wanted most— his father's recognition—had always been out of reach. Whatever the reason, he had never truly felt that this was his home. At the same time, he had always assumed his feelings would be vastly different if he bore his father's name.

But his father had claimed him. A lifelong dream had been fulfilled. And still he felt . . . misplaced.

Dominic stared out at the night, the mists settling over the darkness like the loneliness settling into his heart.

*Sweet heaven, but I miss her.*

Remi's face swam before him, a soft smile on her lips, her honey-blond hair curling wildly about her shoulders. He longed to reach out and take her in his arms. To touch her again, to kiss her. These now were his dreams.

Dreams he would never see fulfilled if he lived four lifetimes.

BY THE TIME Dominic returned the next day from helping bury the men fallen while defending the king, his mother was waiting for him in one of the ante-rooms. He stopped upon entering, slightly taken aback because it resembled the room where he had first seen Remi.

"My father?" He removed his mantle and set it on a nearby chair. "Does his health improve?"

"I am most pleased to report that it does. He took nourishment this morning and now rests comfort-ably. And you, my son," Alise said, watching him closely. "How do you fare this day?"

"I am well."

"And are you happy?"

He smiled. "I am happy for you. Although I must admit, to return and find one's mother married after so many years was disquieting."

"I suppose it must seem so to you."

Dominic glanced at her left hand and noticed that she wore a plain gold wedding band. "The ring you gave me—"

"Is a match for the one William wears. He took it off when he thought I had betrayed him."

"And you did the same." Somehow, Dominic knew the removal of both rings had occurred at the same time. The day he and his mother arrived at Kerwick Castle.

"Yes. But it was right for you to have it."

"You must have loved him for so long. Had you given up hope that you would ever be together?"

"I have always known this happiness waited for me."

"How could you have known?"

"The same way you know where your happiness waits."

Dominic looked away. "I do not dwell on such things."

"Ah, but you must."

"I would speak of other things, Mother," he insisted, a hard edge in his voice.

"Very well." Alise walked toward the door.

"Wait."

She stopped.

"Forgive me, Mother. I . . . please, do not go."

Silently, she turned to face him.

"Mother, I must ask you something." When she still did not speak, he began to pace. "I have always known you were . . . different. Special. We never talked of it, but I knew. Now, I must ask . . ." He ceased pacing and ran his hands through his hair. "Are you . . . are you . . ."

"Nay," she said so softly her voice barely carried. "I am not a witch."

Dominic's eyes widened. "How . . . how?"

"I am Learned. There is a difference."

Shaken to his very foundation, Dominic sat down in the chair for fear his legs might not continue to support him. "'Tis one thing to wonder. Another to know for sure."

"And do you love me less?"

His gaze met hers and he was surprised to see fear and uncertainty in her eyes. "If you are Learned, surely you know the answer. You are my mother, I love you no less."

Alise sighed. "I cannot see everything."

"But you can *see* . . . the future?" He had to know if Remi was all right. As painful as it would be to ask, he had to know.

Alise came closer and touched his cheek with the back of her hand. "She is well, my son, this one who wears your ring. Lonely, but well."

Dominic grabbed his mother's hand. "God's teeth, you can read my thoughts."

"Nay, but I can feel your pain. Only love brings such sorrow."

"Aye," he said after a moment. "There is pain. I must face living the rest of my life without the woman I love. Missing half of my heart, my soul. I speak, I eat, I see sunrise and moonrise, but I am as dead as those brave knights we laid to rest."

"But you have the long-sought desire of your heart. William has publicly recognized you as his son and rightful heir. It is as you have always wished, is it not?"

"Aye, and I am grateful, and praise God that my father lives, but . . ."

"But what?"

"But I *miss her*."

"And if you could be with her again?"

Dominic closed his eyes. "Even love cannot conquer time."

"The past and the future come together in love. But you must decide."

"You speak in riddles."

"I know where you have been these past days."

His eyes popped open. "You *saw* me?"

"It was not necessary. I sent you."

Dominic came out of his chair. "You sent me?"

"To be precise, I sent the book so that you could be called."

"The book? *Rogues Across Time*," he whispered. "Why?"

"Many reasons. Some that have nothing to do with you, but much to do with what will happen in the world. If you had remained in battle against Richard's men, you would have died. If you had died, you would not have saved the king. And if the king had died, there would be consequences that would eventually reshape the world long into the future."

"So you have always known everything that would happen?"

"Not everything. There is always a choice to be made."

"What choice?"

"You could have stayed with the woman you love."

"Aye." He did not want to admit how close he had come to doing so. How close he had come to forsaking honor for love.

"You still have a choice," she told him. "To live in this time, an honored son with land and title. Or you could forfeit all you have to return to her."

All that he had. Would he forfeit all that he had?

What did he have without Remi?

He thought about his mother and was glad she had found her happiness, but that was her life, not his. He was humbled to at last have the father he longed for, but even that victory rang hollow without Remi at his side. The home he had longed to call his own felt foreign. By his own admission, he had always felt like a *misfit*. A man in the wrong place. And the wrong time.

What did he have without Remi?

Nothing.

"Aye," he told his mother at last. "I would gladly forfeit everything." He shook his head. "But it is not possible."

The Duchess of Kerwick put her finger beneath her son's chin and tilted his face up. "And what would you say if I told you that love," she said smiling, "makes all things possible?"

*The Present*

"YOU BUSY?" Clint Hogan asked, sticking his head into Remi's office after a quick knock.

"Nope. C'mon in." Actually, she was glad to have someone to talk to. Maybe she could stop thinking about Dominic for two seconds. Something she hadn't been able to do since he left.

"Hey, you okay?"

"Sure," she lied.

"You look kinda tired."

"Who doesn't around here?" She glanced away, hoping he didn't mention her puffy eyes or slightly red nose. By-products of a tear-filled, sleepless night.

"You got that right."

"Did you need something?"

"Oh, yeah. I almost forgot. We're short one kidnap victim for tonight's show. Can you fill in?"

"Oh, damn," she said wearily. "I'm not up for this."

"Sorry, but Ruthann called in ten minutes ago from the emergency room. One of her kids fell out of a treehouse and needs stitches."

"Ouch." Remi winced. "Isn't anyone else available?"

"Not a single solitary soul."

The words *single* and *solitary* rang inside her head like echoes down an empty hall. Single, meaning not two. Solitary, meaning alone. So alone.

"Okay," she relented. "Guess you've got yourself a victim."

Well, she thought as Clint left, at least it will prolong going home to an empty house.

Of course, that didn't solve her problem of facing that same empty house the next night or the night after that. It didn't come anywhere near solving the problem of lying awake, staring at the ceiling of her bedroom, remembering . . . remembering . . .

She held her left hand up and the silver in her ring glinted in the harsh light of her office, in the harsh light of reality. A reality without Dominic. The ring was her only tangible link to him since the copy of *Rogues Across Time* had vanished after the performance. She recalled placing the book on the corner of her desk that night, but now it was either lost or simply . . . gone. Maybe it was just as well, Remi thought. Having it around, being able to gaze at the drawing of Dominic anytime she pleased would be sheer torture.

The memories were torture enough. But agony or not, she couldn't—wouldn't—shut them out. They were all she had of him. So, she clung to them, relived them over and over, no matter how painful the reliving.

Dominic had been gone only a couple of days, yet it seemed like years had passed since she'd felt his lips on hers, his arms holding her close. In that brief span of time, she had made some discoveries about herself that would have shocked her a week ago.

Namely, that the security she had longed for wasn't a place.

It was a person. Actually, two people.

Dominic, and the person she had become by loving him.

For as long as she could remember, she had looked at her parents' way of life and made a conscious decision to go the other direction. She thought that because they lived a vagabond existence, something was missing, that they had no stability. Poor fool that she was, she didn't even understand that they loved each other so much that where they were never mattered—just as long as they were together.

Well, she understood now. Loving Dominic had brought that understanding. He had not only changed her physically, showing her what real sensuality was, he had changed who she was, what she thought, how she looked at the world.

But what good was anything without him? She missed him so. Her arms ached for him.

"Knock it off," she said, swiping at her tear-drenched face. She dressed in her costume and headed toward the arena. Thank goodness, she wasn't having to do the sorceress again. She couldn't face it tonight. In fact, she didn't think she could face doing that part again, ever.

"You ready?" one of the actor/Saracens asked as she approached the staging area.

"I was born ready," Remi quipped.

"Okay, when I say go, grab the saddle horn," he instructed, twining rope around her hands to make it look as if she were bound. "I'll have you around your waist and I promise not to drop you but once."

Remi eyed her would-be kidnapper. "That's a comfort."

"Piece of cake," he told her. "Then we do the slave-girl-struggle thing. One of the guys comes out, swoops you up, then gently sets you down over by the railing. Does the courtly-bow thing. You know the drill."

"Is there a quiz later?"

"Naw, we just hang you by your thumbnails if you screw up."

"And I was worried."

He gave her fake bindings a pat. "You're good to go." Then he mounted his horse as Remi stepped up onto a wooden box so the actor wouldn't have too far to reach. He clasped her around the waist, gave the signal they were ready and rode into the arena with his captive.

Everything went as scripted. Remi struggled and the Saracens did their thing. Finally, it was time for the Crusader Knight to rescue the damsel in distress. As the victim, Remi was stranded on a perch made to look like a huge rock, while three of the Saracens went off to do battle with three crusaders. Her back was to the entrance, but even without seeing, she knew the brief blare of trumpets signaled the rescue to begin.

Unlike the scene where the Black Knight comes through a screen of smoke, the Crusader Knight was supposed to ride in through the arena entrance right after the trumpets sounded. But he didn't.

Somebody was dillydallying around, Remi decided. A second blare of trumpets. Then she heard the sound of a horse's hooves, and was relieved her rescuer had finally picked up on his cue.

The thundering of hooves came closer. The crowd gave a wild cheer, as expected, when the crusader galloped into the spotlight. Only the cheer didn't last as long as usual. For just a second, Remi looked over her shoulder, and saw why. The knight wasn't a crusader at all. They had the wrong guy riding in to save her.

"Great," she said under her breath. She turned her attention back to the battling knights and waited. .

She heard the knight coming on. Obviously it was too late to change now. She only hoped the audience didn't complain about having the wrong knight in the wrong time period.

He was close now. So close, she could hear the horse's heavy breathing. A second before she felt the knight's arm at her waist, Remi glanced back.

And saw a knight in full black armor, astride a huge, black-as-midnight war-horse bearing down on her like Satan coming for the last soul on earth.

Her mouth opened to issue the scripted scream, but nothing came out but air as the knight's powerful arm clamped around her waist and she was slammed against his body. The stallion reared, his legs thrashing the air, and any second, Remi fully expected to find herself unceremoniously dumped on her rear.

The knight reined in the horse, hauling her up and across his lap. But instead of galloping to the far side of the arena, he rode out of the spotlight and out of the arena.

"Just what in—" In a blur, she saw the knight's helmet go sailing off. "Sam Hill do you think—"

Recognition came a heartbeat before his mouth took hers.

Remi threw her arms around his neck and herself into the kiss. A kiss she thought never to know again.

"Dominic! Dominic!" she cried, tears streaming down her face. "Is it really you? Oh, God, please don't let me be dreaming."

"'Tis no dream, love." He kissed her wet cheeks, her eyes, her nose.

"But how? Never mind, I don't even care." She drew back to look into his beloved face. "You're never leaving me again, do you hear? Never."

"Nay, my sweet witch. Trust me," he promised, holding her closer, knowing that now they had all the time in the world to love each other.

## MILLION DOLLAR SWEEPSTAKES

BRIDE'S BAY RESORT

## UNLOCK THE DOOR TO GREAT ROMANCE AT BRIDE'S BAY RESORT

Join Harlequin's new across-the-lines series, set in an exclusive hotel on an island off the coast of South Carolina.

Seven of your favorite authors will bring you exciting stories about fascinating heroes and heroines discovering love at Bride's Bay Resort.

Look for these fabulous stories coming to a store near you beginning in January 1996.

**Harlequin American Romance #613 in January**
*Matchmaking Baby* by Cathy Gillen Thacker

**Harlequin Presents #1794 in February**
*Indiscretions* by Robyn Donald

**Harlequin Intrigue #362 in March**
*Love and Lies* by Dawn Stewardson

**Harlequin Romance #3404 in April**
*Make Believe Engagement* by Day Leclaire

**Harlequin Temptation #588 in May**
*Stranger in the Night* by Roseanne Williams

**Harlequin Superromance #695 in June**
*Married to a Stranger* by Connie Bennett

**Harlequin Historicals #324 in July**
*Dulcie's Gift* by Ruth Langan

Visit Bride's Bay Resort each month wherever
Harlequin books are sold.

HARLEQUIN ®

BBAYG

HARLEQUIN®

*Temptation*

# Mail Order Men—Satisfaction Guaranteed!

Tanner Jones seems to be the answer to Dori Fitzpatrick's prayers. Ever since her rich ex-husband took her five-year-old son away from her, Dori's been looking for a way to get little Jimmy back. And she needs a husband to do it—preferably one who works for a living. But Dori soon finds out there's more to Tanner than meets the eye.

**#600 HOLDING OUT FOR A HERO**
by Vicki Lewis Thompson

Available in August wherever
Harlequin books are sold.

HARLEQUIN®

*Temptation*

MMEN

# Weddings by DeWilde

Since the turn of the century the elegant and fashionable
DeWilde stores have helped brides around the world
turn the fantasy of their "Special Day" into reality. But now the
store and three generations of family are torn apart by the
separation of Grace and Jeffrey DeWilde. Family members
face new challenges and loves in this fast-paced, glamorous,
internationally set series. For weddings and romance, glamour
and fun-filled entertainment, enter the world of DeWildes...

## Watch for A BRIDE FOR DADDY
## by Leandra Logan
## Coming to you in August 1996

Designer Tessa Montiefiori was determined that her talent, and
not her family connections to the DeWildes, would be her claim
to fame. She'd modeled one of her own wedding gowns as part
of a promotional contest, and her dreams were falling into
place, until two young children decided that Tessa herself was
the prize, and a perfect bride for Daddy....

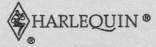

HARLEQUIN ®

Look us up on-line at: http://www.romance.net

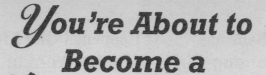

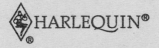